KU-048-220

SONG OF MY HEART

Andi Cox lands her dream job, looking after the two daughters of pop music icon Jas Summers. But when Jas starts arranging a summer charity concert in the grounds of his country house and the girls become the subject of kidnap threats, her troubles really begin . . . Along the way Andi acquires a new stepmother in the eccentric Hermione — and then she loses her heart to Jas . . .

MARGARET MOUNSDON

---◆---

SONG OF MY HEART

Complete and Unabridged

LINFORD
Leicester

First published in Great Britain in 2010

First Linford Edition
published 2011

Copyright © 2010 by Margaret Mounsdon
All rights reserved

British Library CIP Data

Mounsdon, Margaret.
   Song of my heart. - -
   (Linford romance library)
   1. Children of celebrities- -Care- -Fiction.
   2. Rock musicians- -Fiction. 3. Stepmothers
   - -Fiction. 4. Love stories. 5. Large type books.
   I. Title II. Series
   823.9'2–dc22

   ISBN 978–1–4448–0799–8

COVENTRY CITY LIBRARIES

Published by
F. A. Thorpe (Publishing)
Anstey, Leicestershire

Set by Words & Graphics Ltd.
Anstey, Leicestershire
Printed and bound in Great Britain by
T. J. International Ltd., Padstow, Cornwall

This book is printed on acid-free paper

'I Always Love A Challenge'

'Of course I've heard of Jas Summers,' Andi replied with surprise. 'Who hasn't?'

Bill Branch nodded. 'Thought you might have done,' he acknowledged with a wry smile. '*Song Of My Heart* is about the only protest anthem I know all the words to.'

Andi leaned back in her chair. She enjoyed her Monday morning sessions with Bill. With only the two of them in the agency now, they had more or less dispensed with any boss/employee hierarchy. Like everyone else, they had been hit by cutbacks and although business was quiet they were managing to keep their heads above the water.

'Do you know the words to *Song Of My Heart*?' Bill asked.

'Yes,' Andi admitted, remembering her pre-teen disco days when it was cool to be seen wearing Jas Summers' T shirts. 'What has Jas Summers and *Song Of My Heart* got to do with us?' she asked.

'Jas Summers has bought March Manor,' Bill informed her.

For months rumours had been rife about the new owner of the Tudor manor house set in its own vast parklands on the outskirts of the town of Old Haven. March Manor had been put on the market after the last member of the de Vigne family had died. The dowager, Lady de Vigne had been child-less and her closest relatives were distant cousins who lived in South Africa, who had absolutely had no interest in taking on the residency of a crumbling pile of ancient stones.

Various buyer names had been bandied around, from a famous foot-baller to a television personality, even a junior royal had been mentioned. Now it seemed none of them had been right.

'So it's true?' Andi said.

'What is?'

'I was watching breakfast television yesterday morning and they ran a story about Jas Summers wanting to return to this country from America after the break up of his marriage to Bella Ross. They mentioned his interest in a Tudor property in the Kent countryside.'

'And you put two and two together?'

'I did wonder, yes. I mean there aren't that many Tudor manor houses for sale in our neck of the woods.'

'Fan of Jas Summers, are you?' Bill asked.

Andi gave a shamefaced smile. Jas Summers, the former bad boy of pop was the voice of a generation. Students had chanted his songs as they marched in protest against authority and injustices, and his signature song, *Song Of My Heart* was the anthem of the oppressed. He was an active human rights campaigner too and no rally was complete unless Jas Summers was involved somewhere along the line.

'He's twelve years older than me so a bit before my time,' Andi said, 'but his music is ageless, so yes, I suppose I am a closet fan of his.'

'Good, because you are going to get the chance to work for him.'

'What?' Andi jerked her elbow and spilt tea all over her desk. She mopped it up with a tissue. 'Would you mind repeating that?'

She could not have been more surprised if Bill had suggested security for the astronauts on a trip to the moon.

'Jas Summers has requested our services,' he repeated.

'Is this some kind of joke?' Andi demanded.

Andi stared at Bill in amazement. While her boss's integrity was of the highest and the service his security firm provided totally professional, they had downsized drastically to keep pace with the economic climate and there was no way the two of them were into providing personal protection for the likes of Jas Summers. Jas Summers was a big ticket.

Like all stars of his status he had received threats to his safety. His lifestyle demanded round-the-clock surveillance.

'With all due respect, Bill, you are on the wrong side of fifty to be of any use to Jas, and as for me what good would I be to him — twenty-four, slim, female? A determined average fan could flatten me without even trying. Besides which surely Jas Summers has his own personal security team?'

'I realise working for Jas Summers would tax your skills to the limit, but I wouldn't have suggested you for the post if I didn't think you could do it.'

'But why would Jas Summers want me on his staff?' Andi still could not get her head round Bill's news. 'He could choose virtually anyone in the world.'

'People trust you, Andi. You're not a heavyweight. They feel comfortable with you and that's why I know you'll be ideal for this job.'

'What exactly does it entail?' Andi asked warily. 'I can think of nothing worse than looking after Jas Summers himself. He's not exactly renowned for his reliability.'

Every detail of Jas's life before he became famous had been the subject of numerous articles and interviews. He was the youngest of a tribe of children who grew up on the west coast of Ireland.

He barely went to school. Jas Summers more often than not had bunked off lessons and hung around the town with a rough crowd. He had received most of his education from the school of life and along the way he had suffered more than his fair share of hard knocks.

Although marriage and fatherhood had mellowed his image over the years, Andi suspected if he was backed into a corner he could still take good care of himself without any help from her.

He was tall and well built and needed to keep up his stamina for his gruelling schedule of concerts. She had no doubt he could probably still pack a mean punch. In the old days he had never shied away from confrontation.

'As you know,' Bill was speaking again, 'old Lady de Vigne only lived in a small part of the manor and the rest of the building fell into disrepair. It's going to need a lot of work doing to it to get it habitable. Jas wants to move in as soon as possible. He's prepared to rough it but he's got two daughters and he wants someone to help look after them.'

'Wouldn't a nanny be more suited to the job?'

'Agreed, but Bella Ross his ex-wife wants to be in on any interviews. Now she can't get over here until later in the summer. They have joint custody of the girls but she's taken on a new commission in the Far East. Their current nanny will be leaving to get married, so Jas and the girls will be arriving in this country from America at the end of next week. Jas thought it would be a good idea for them to have a suitable female presence in their life but not necessarily a nanny.'

'I still don't see why he doesn't use his own people. He's got a vast army of staff hasn't he?'

'Jas is keen to integrate into the community and where possible he wants to use local resources. All the proposed work on March Manor will be carried out by firms based in the area. Of course he has his own team of advisers, but they have been instructed to sound out the community and where possible make use of the services on offer.'

'That's quite some mission statement.' Andi grinned at the serious look on her boss's face. 'Did you dream it up on your own?' she asked in an attempt to lighten the atmosphere.

Bill's weathered face softened into an answering smile. 'Actually I'm reading it out from an e-mail his agent sent me. Sounds good, doesn't it? Now what's your take on the situation?'

Andi made a face. 'To be honest, Bill, I'm not keen on the idea. Don't get me wrong, I'm sure Jas is a wonderful father and Bella Ross is an equally great mother, but they are,' she hesitated, 'how can I put this?'

'Media royalty?'

'Exactly. Their daughters, besides being spoilt, are probably also traumatised by the stress of their parents' divorce. They are being uprooted from their home, flown half way across the world, to live in a crumbling old ruin that along with the rest of their life is falling down around their ears. Who could blame them for feeling mixed up? They'll need professional counselling, not the services of a lightweight security guard trying to masquerade as a nanny.'

'Here's a picture of them.'

Bill slid a grainy print across the desk towards her. The younger child wearing a striped summer dress and beaming at the camera was missing several teeth.

She was blonde and had an impish smile that suggested she would never take life too seriously. Andi smiled back reluctantly, then her eyes strayed to her older sister. She caught her breath. The pose was challenging and Andi knew instantly this girl was trouble. Her eyes betrayed a knowledge of life far beyond her years.

Andi could see a resemblance to her father in the way her stance challenged authority. In his younger days, Jas Summers would have adopted a similar confrontational pose for the camera.

'I know what you're going to say,' Bill spoke first, 'but before you do, there's a little family history you ought to know about.'

'What's to know?' Andi pushed the photo back across the desk. 'I grant you, the younger child is a sweetie, but the older one would run rings round me. How old is she?'

'Sixteen.'

'That makes her only eight years younger than me and judging by that picture I should think a million times more worldly.'

'Don't put yourself down, Andi.'

'I'm not, Bill, but think on it. She's

10

grown up with every luxury money can buy. She's sophisticated way beyond her years. She's got a superstar father and an equally successful mother who runs her own image consultancy and who, before her marriage, was the daughter of an Irish peer. She chooses not to use her title, but that doesn't stop her being a member of the aristocracy. My security experience is much more low key, more along the lines of escorting children to school, looking after frail senior citizens and calming down the occasional domestic disturbance.'

'What do you think of the younger child?' Bill asked.

Andi hesitated. 'She's lovely,' she admitted.

'She's also adopted.'

'That explains the lack of resemblance to Jas Summers or Bella Ross.'

'She's Jas's sister's child. They were very close and when his sister died Jas adopted her daughter.'

'Heart-warming though it is, I still don't see what influence that bit of information will have on my decision.'

'None at all, I suppose.' Bill looked disappointed. 'So you're really not interested in the job?'

'I'm sorry if you feel I've let you down, Bill, only I honestly feel I couldn't do justice to the assignment. It's a high profile placing and any adverse publicity would reflect badly on us and we do have the reputation of the agency to consider.' Andi paused. 'We're batting out of our league here.'

'That's a great pity.' Bill frowned then cleared his throat, as if uncertain what to say next.

'There's more isn't there?' Andi asked her suspicions aroused. 'Something you are not telling me?' she pushed.

'Jas is anxious for the post to be taken up almost immediately. You are available and he is offering a more than generous fee, and I forgot to mention there'll be a luxury camper van at your disposal which would mean you wouldn't have to sleep in the manor.'

'It's not a question of money or camper vans, although I'm not saying both wouldn't come in handy,' Andi added with a wry smile.

Her present accommodation was only temporary and Andi would need to start looking for a new flat in the not too distant future, but she hardly thought a camper van, luxury status or not, was exactly what she was looking for.

'Surely you're up to the challenge of looking after two girls,' Bill used his coaxing voice on her. 'I mean what can they do to you?'

'There speaks a man who's never had daughters. Bill, you'd be surprised. In my experience teenage girls are capable of any skulduggery and if things should go wrong, you can bet your bottom dollar Jas Summers won't go blaming his daughters. I'll be the fall guy every time.'

'The younger one is only seven years old.'

'When push comes to shove, who is

13

she going to side with, me or the big sister she probably idolises? Bill, I'll be enemy number one and I can do without that sort of hassle in my life.'

'Perhaps it was unfair of me to spring it on you,' he agreed. 'Only . . . ' he hesitated as if uncertain how to go on.

Andi leaned forward. 'Come on, out with it.'

'You'll have to know sooner rather than later,' Bill admitted, screwing up his face as though he were in some sort of pain.

'Know what?' Andi's interest quickened. 'You're not ill are you?' Now she came to look at him properly she realised he was a bit pale.

'No, it's nothing like that, but ever since Jackie died, my son has been pestering me to join him and his family in New Zealand. They've got enough room in their house, and after last winter's cold weather, well, I'm seriously thinking about it. I didn't want to worry you about this earlier, but for the first time ever in the history of the

14

agency, we aren't making a profit and to put it frankly things can't carry on like this.'

'You're not selling up?' Andi was aghast.

'I have had a good offer. Of course I wouldn't dream of accepting it unless you were properly settled, Andi, you know that.'

'Don't be ridiculous,' Andi protested, 'moving to New Zealand is a marvellous opportunity and you absolutely have to do it and take up the offer on the agency, now, before they change their mind.'

'But I wouldn't want to leave you in the lurch. The buyers have told me they can't guarantee you a job in the new set up. I couldn't do that to you, Andi. At times I wouldn't have been able to run the agency without you. I owe you a tremendous debt.'

'Which you have just paid back by offering me a marvellous job that will see me in rich pickings for years.'

'That's not how you were telling it a

few moment's ago,' Bill pointed out.

'You know me,' Andi tossed back her tawny brown hair, 'I always love a challenge. Don't you remember that's why you took me on in the first place?'

Andi had been a gawky seventeen years old when she had applied for the job at Bill Branch's agency. There was something about her bravado that had appealed to him. Jackie, his wife, had liked her too and despite Andi's lack of experience they had relied on their instincts and taken her on.

Andi had never given either of them the slightest cause to regret their decision, and when Bill had been widowed, he had grown closer to Andi, relying on her more as a friend than an employee.

'If you're absolutely sure?' Bill asked hopefully, 'I wouldn't want to pressure you into making the wrong decision.'

'I've never been more certain of anything in my life.'

Andi hoped her smile wouldn't betray the deep sense of uncertainty she

16

was feeling inside. She didn't want this job. Playing nanny to the children of superstars was not the sort of work she enjoyed, but she supposed there were plenty of worse ways to earn a living and there was no way she was going to scupper Bill's plans for his future.

'Now you get that e-mail off to Jas Summers accepting his offer and don't worry, Bill. If life gets too dire at March Manor, I'll drive off into the sunset in Jas's camper van and join you in New Zealand.'

'You know,' Bill's glasses worked their way down his nose, 'you'd be more than welcome. I'm sure my son could find room for you somewhere. I should have thought of that before.'

Not given to sentimentality Andi had difficulty swallowing the lump in her throat. When you're seventeen and your life is in a mess, knights on white chargers don't appear very often. Bill had been her white knight and saved the day, but it was time Andi stopped relying on him.

'Thanks, Bill. Take a rain check on that one?'

Parting from Bill would be a wrench, but Andi was twenty-four years old. Perhaps her life needed to be taken in a new direction. Whatever her future held, she had no doubt life with Jas Summers would be anything but dull.

A Meeting at the Manor

Andi's taxi bumped along the country lane leading to March Manor. Over the past two weeks she had managed to condense her life into two suitcases and a large bin bag. Various dues had been called in on old friends, who had taken care of the few bits of furniture Andi had acquired during her brief engagement to Tony Strong.

Her eyes clouded over. These days she hardly thought about her ex-fiancé at all, but at the time, his disloyalty had almost been more than she could bear. She'd fallen for the oldest line in the book.

Policemen often worked unsocial hours so she'd had no reason to disbelieve him, until his overtime knocked on the flat door one Sunday afternoon and informed Andi of the exact nature of Tony's demanding work schedule.

Andi's one broken engagement had convinced her that when it came to matters of the heart, in future she was going to have to be a lot more careful in her choice of men.

'Part of Jas Summers' team are you?' The taxi driver broke into her thoughts as they neared March Manor.

Luckily he was the breed of driver who didn't need a reply. 'I've been up and down this road so many times over the past week, the car could almost make its way there without any help from me.' He revealed a set of dazzling white teeth. 'You've never seen anything like it.'

'Is that so?' Andi murmured wondering not for the first time exactly what she had let herself in for.

'Yes.' He warmed to his theme. 'Last week there was some sort of refurbishment meeting at the manor, all sorts of important officials with bulging bags of paperwork descended on the place. Then there are plans for the grounds to be landscaped and a whole lot more planning permission's going to be needed for that one too.

'The pond's being cleaned then re-stocked. That Jas Summers is going to have a job and a half on his hands here. Still, it will be good for the local community. Using local labour whenever he can, I've heard. Good man. I approve of that. Here we are then.'

A security guard emerged from a small cabin at the gate and strolled towards them.

'Hi Al,' the taxi driver greeted him, 'young lady passenger for you. Going to the big house.'

The guard acknowledged the greeting with a pleasant smile. 'Do you have a letter of introduction, Madam?' he asked.

Andi produced her paperwork and the guard returned to his cabin and made a telephone call.

'Go straight on in, Miss Cox,' the guard re-emerged from his hut. 'You're expected.' After he pressed some numbers into a dial pad attached to the wrought iron gates they creaked open slowly.

'Another half mile or so of drive to go.' The taxi driver engaged gear. 'Still at least this part of the road is made up. First thing Jas Summers did was to have it seen to. Not before time either. I tell you, after last winter's storms, the road was like a quagmire.'

Andi's heart began to beat a nervous tattoo. It was too late to back out now even if she had wanted to. Bill's plans to move to New Zealand were well under way. His son had already sent him an air ticket, and Andi's landlady had been pleased to learn she was moving on.

'Not that you haven't been an ideal tenant, dear,' she explained, 'but I had promised my sister that my niece could have the room when she starts college in the autumn. Going to work for Jas Summers are you?' she enquired with a concerned smile. 'I hope you know what you're letting yourself in for.'

Andi hoped so too. If things went wrong at March Manor, she didn't know what she would do.

Her parents had separated when she was a child and her mother had moved to Scotland on her re-marriage. Andi's brother was ten years older than her and they had never been close. His work took him all over the country and she wasn't exactly sure where he was at the present time.

As for her father, Andi bit her lip, she had meant to get down to the coast to see him before she moved to March Manor, but there really hadn't been time. On her first free day she vowed she would pay him a visit, but right now her top priority was to settle in to her new job and take each day at a time.

'Lovely house, isn't it?' The taxi driver paused as the car swung round a rhododendron bush.

There in front of them stood March Manor. Andi had never seen it in the flesh before. Although she had lived in Old Haven all the time she had been working for Bill Branch, visits to March Manor had not been on the agenda.

Lady de Vigne had turned into something of a recluse in her latter years and visitors to the manor were discouraged, not that she would have had much use for a security guard anyway.

It was indeed a lovely house. Andi gasped as she looked up at the ivyclad building. Various members of the de Vigne family had added to the original structure, which according to local legend had been built during the reign of the Tudors.

As the family fortunes soared and dipped, according to which member of the family was currently in favour at court, work on the manor was a bit of a haphazard affair, with the result that several wings of the house were more developed than others, all of which added to its individual charm.

Several vehicles were parked on the hard standing outside the stone steps leading up to the house and as her driver drew up the front door opened.

'Well I never,' the taxi driver gasped,

'he's never done that before. You are honoured, Miss. First time I've known him to personally greet a visitor.' He swung round to take a good look at her. 'You're not a member of the family are you?'

'No,' Andi shook her head, 'and before you ask I'm not famous either. How much do I owe you for the fare?'

'That's all been taken care of.' The taxi driver leapt out of his seat and opened her door.

Andi longed to be in the position to decline the offer, but it wasn't a wise move when your bank manager was writing urgent letters suggesting meetings to discuss the future of your finances. Ever since the break up of her engagement, Andi's financial situation had dipped alarmingly.

She looked up at the man walking towards her. She would have recognised him anywhere. Jas Summers was taller than she had expected, and his hair was showing the slightest wing of grey at the sides but there was no mistaking the charismatic smile of welcome, or the eyes, which could speak volumes.

Jas was wearing a casual checked shirt and denims that looked as though they had seen better days.

'How do you do?' he extended a hand. 'My name is Jas Summers,' he introduced himself. 'You must be Miss Cox. I'm very pleased to meet you.'

The voice was raspy, but it held all the warmth of a man who was genuinely pleased to see her.

'Yes, I am,' Andi fluttered taken on the hop. She hadn't expected Jas to be quite so normal.

'Thank you,' he acknowledged the driver who was hovering around in the background. 'Bob, isn't it?'

'Yes, sir.' Bob looked suitably impressed.

'Sorry we haven't had a chance to meet up before now, but thanks for all your help. I know I've created a lot of extra work for you, but I want you to also know it's appreciated.'

'My pleasure, sir.' Bob tipped his cap.

'Catch up later?' Jas suggested.

Andi smiled as she watched Bob drive off in a daze. No doubt the story of how he met the superstar would be doing the rounds within moments of him arriving back at the depot.

Jas turned his attention back to Andi. He looked down at her suitcases and then up to the bulging bin liner in her arms. The expression in his eyes changed and Andi hoped he wasn't having second thoughts about employing her. She was well aware she couldn't hold a candle to the efficient team of uniformed security guards who patrolled the grounds twenty four seven, but she was willing to give this job her best shot.

'Is this your luggage?' Jas asked, unable to keep the surprise out of his voice.

Andi tossed back her head in challenge. 'In my business it's a good idea to travel light,' she replied.

Jas's lips softened into his trademark slightly crooked smile.

'I wish you'd try telling my female relations that one.' He still had the faintest trace of an Irish accent in his voice but it had been honed by so many years of living in America.

'Yes, well, if you'll show me where to put my bags I can start work immediately,' Andi said, wishing she had paid a tad more attention to her appearance.

Before helping her landlady clean her room in preparation for the decorators who were moving in the following day, Andi had packed most of her work clothes away. She hadn't expected Jas Summers to actually greet her on arrival and that morning had thrown on a casual blouse and summer printed skirt.

The driver had arrived to collect her earlier than she had expected and there hadn't been time to shampoo her hair either. Aware it was too late to do anything about her appearance now, Andi did her best to present a professional image, which wasn't easy when you were clutching a bin liner full of dirty washing.

'There's no need to start work yet,' Jas replied. 'The girls haven't actually arrived so you can have the day off.'

Aware of a man and woman hovering behind her, Andi turned round.

'Ivy,' she gasped in surprise recognising the older woman. 'What are you doing here?'

The next moment she was enveloped in a huge hug that almost took her breath away.

'Hello, love.' The man by Ivy's side tried to get in on the action, but Ivy elbowed him out of the way.

'Me and Harry were so grateful for all Andi did,' Ivy explained to Jas over Andi's head. 'Our youngest granddaughter was being bullied something dreadful, but the gang soon left her alone after Andi took over the job of escorting her to school every day.'

'Sorry, Mr Summers,' Andi apologised to Jas as she managed to extricate herself from Ivy's embrace, 'Ivy and Harry are old friends.'

'That's quite all right, Miss Cox,' he responded solemnly, 'don't let me interrupt your reunion.'

'Your daughters will be in good hands with Andi,' Ivy assured him.

'Yes, I'm sure,' Jas acknowledged. 'The camper's parked round the back. It's only just been delivered so the keys are still in it. Let's go and see it.

'Ivy and Harry are living in a cottage in the grounds so you'll probably be seeing a lot more of them. I suggest you leave things as they are for the moment.'

Andi nodded, still not entirely sure what was going on. The last she'd heard Ivy and Harry were moving home to be nearer to their daughter, the mother of the granddaughter who was being bullied. Obviously their plans must have changed.

'Come on,' Jas urged her before Andi could think things through, 'let's have some tea, then I'll take you on a guided tour of March Manor, not that there's much to see as yet. I've had the kitchen done out so we can at least eat and drink in comfort, but as for the rest of the property, well, it's in a bit of a mess as you can see from my appearance.'

He dusted down his jeans and shook his head and Andi saw that what she thought were grey hairs was in fact a film of dust.

'Part of the ceiling came down on me while I was trying to take some measurements,' Jas explained. 'I opened the window before I choked and that's when I saw you arrive. Er,' he hesitated, 'I don't have to keep calling you Miss Cox, do I?' he asked with a look of concern.

For someone of superstar status, Jas was surprisingly polite, Andi thought reluctantly. She had been prepared for confrontation but all she had received from him so far was courtesy and kindness.

'It's Andi,' she said, adding, 'short for Andromeda.'

'A woman of incredible beauty who lived among the stars,' Jas replied.

31

'Rather apt wouldn't you say?'

Before Andi could comment on this puzzling remark, he said, 'We're all very informal here. I'm Jas to one and all, Andi, so come on.' Very casually he took hold of her hand. 'The guided tour starts here.' He paused before they entered the hall, 'by the way, you have to wear one of these. Mega important. That rule goes for everyone so don't let the girls give you any stick about it. No hat, no entry. Got it?'

He rammed a yellow hard hat on her head. 'There. Not the most glamorous of headwear, but we don't want you being injured on your first day in the new job, do we?'

Jas took hold of her hand again. 'Off we go. Safety in numbers,' he added sidling along the skirting board. 'Follow me and mind your footing. In places the flooring is as dicey as the ceiling.'

'Are you doing the renovations yourself?' she asked.

'I like to keep my hand in. My father was a builder so I suppose it's in my genes. Think the gang feel I'm being a bit of a nuisance at times, but what the heck? I'm paying the bills.' He flashed her a brief smile. 'Now are we ready?'

Still unable to believe superstar Jas Summers was clutching her hand Andi let him lead her through a pile of rubble and into the kitchen for a cup of tea.

Andi Begins Her Job With Jas

'Builders' tea do you?' Jas asked as Andi settled down at the huge pine table.

'Help yourself.' He nudged a fruit-cake at her. 'No need to stand on ceremony. Well, you can if you like, but you won't get anything to eat. Greedy as gannets most of the crew here.' He waved a tea caddy in the air. 'Builders tea?' he blinked at her. Andi noticed he had incredibly long eyelashes. The sun streaming through the kitchen window turned them from dark brown to gold. 'I've already asked that, haven't I?' A smile tugged the corners of Jas's mouth. 'Er, did you reply?'

'Strong tea will be fine,' Andi replied. 'Do you want me to make it?'

'If there's one thing I can do after years on the road it is make a good cup of tea,' he insisted. 'I tell you, you haven't lived 'til you've travelled countrywide in a bus full of session men and roadies.

Tea was the only thing that kept me sane — that and my music.'

'I love *Song Of My Heart*,' Andi began, then blushed like a schoolgirl. How could she have said anything so stupid and unoriginal?

'Do you really?' Jas's face lit up. 'I love it when people say that to me. Do you know I wrote it straight off one afternoon on the beach? It was too cold to go swimming and everyone was moaning about the weather. I picked up a pencil and some paper, wrapped myself in a towel and wrote about all the things I loved. I got sand everywhere.' He laughed. 'I'll have a piece of cake if you're cutting a slice,' he said.

Andi picked up a knife and cut two healthy slices of moist cake. 'One of Ivy's finest?' she asked inhaling the twin tangs of orange peel and the lemon zest that Ivy always used in her cake recipes.

Jas nodded and sat down opposite Andi while the jug kettle boiled.

'They're lifesavers, those two. The couple I had originally employed let me down, but Ivy and Harry were available at short notice so I snapped them up before someone else did.'

Andi mumbled a response through a mouthful of fruitcake. She wondered what had gone wrong with Ivy's plans, but as it wasn't in her nature to gossip she finished her slice of cake while Jas poured boiling water onto the tea and left it to draw.

'When do you expect your daughters to arrive?' Andi asked.

'I came on ahead. Bella's flying in with the girls the day after tomorrow. She'll be in transit to the Far East so she won't be coming through Customs. I don't suppose you'll meet her. I've arranged for a member of staff to escort them through passport control, so I suggest you go and collect them from the airport, that way you can introduce yourself. It might help break the ice between you girls if Dad isn't hovering around getting in the way, don't you think? I'll make sure the airline knows who you are and that you have my full authority to collect them.'

The hazel eyes questioned hers.

'That's fine with me,' Andi agreed. 'I'm looking forward to meeting them.'

'Hope you feel the same way in a week's time,' Jas joked.

'Can I ask some questions?'

'Fire away.' Jas leaned back in his chair, 'I've got a few of my own, but ladies first.'

'Your two daughters are called Misty and Holly aren't they?'

'Yes, well no,' Jas amended. Andi looked up from her notes. 'Misty's real name is Mavreen. She was born on a typical Irish morning and Bella and I held her in our arms and watched the sun break through the mist together and the name sort of stuck. It was quite a romantic moment,' Jas said softly, 'the birth of our first child. Bella and I weren't much more than children ourselves and here we were responsible for another human being. It was a life sobering moment.'

For a fleeting moment, Andi felt a

pang of envy. She had imagined such a moment with Tony her ex fiancé, until his 'work commitments' had taken him away from her.

'Misty was so beautiful. She still is, of course,' Jas added with a shamefaced smile. 'Sorry, always go a bit sentimental on that one. Too much information?'

'Not at all.'

The more Andi got to know of Jas Summers the more she began to like him. Superstardom appeared to have left him unchanged. He was simply a man reminiscing over the birth of his first child treasuring the memory of a magic moment with his wife. Again Andi wondered what could have gone wrong between him and Bella Ross.

Bella Ross was beautiful and talented and an immensely successful businesswoman, exactly the right sort of wife for Jas. Admittedly their social backgrounds were different. Bella's parents were Irish aristocracy, but apart from that she and Jas appeared to be soul mates.

'Holly was born on Christmas Day.' Jas was speaking again. His hazel eyes clouded over as he explained. 'She's actually my sister's child, but she was a single parent,' Jas shrugged, 'so we adopted her. Later there were a lot of other issues involved.'

'It's the girls' general background I'm interested in,' Andi put in hastily, returning her attention to the matter in hand.

'What else do you need to know?'

Bill had told Andi Jas's sister had died when Holly was a baby, but Andi decided any other personal information on Holly's mother was on a need-to-know basis only. She cleared her throat.

'Don't think I'm prying, Mr, er I mean, Jas, but you and your wife are divorced?'

'We are, but it was a very amicable parting of the ways. No ripping up of clothes or posting each other's love letters to the press for publication. The girls are our first priority. They're both at pretty delicate stages of their lives and we're determined their welfare won't suffer from the changed situation. As far as they are concerned their parents are always there for them.'

'Why did you decide to uproot everyone and move to March Manor?'

'Bella has business contacts in this country and was thinking of moving back. After so many years in America I felt the urge to come home too, so it was a mutual decision to move back. March Manor came on the market at exactly the right time. The girls will live here with me until Bella is properly settled and everyone's happy about that. As it's the summer, there won't be any schooling or college to worry about yet. I'm only sorry I couldn't start work on March Manor earlier, but I had other commitments.'

'What would my duties entail? I mean you have a full time security team of your own, you don't really need another security guard do you?'

Andi held her breath as Jas wriggled uncomfortably in his chair as if he were about to deliver some unwelcome news. She hoped he wasn't going to say he'd had a re-think on that one and agreed with her and that the whole thing was a huge mistake.

'How can I put this without sounding rude?' He frowned.

'My ego doesn't bruise easily,' Andi informed him.

'The security team here is professional,' Jas blurted out.

'And I'm not — professional?' Andi's mouth curved into a generous smile.

'I haven't offended you?' Jas looked anxious.

'Not at all. I've always been, I suppose you could say, a paid amateur. Bill sent me on courses, that sort of thing and I got a few certificates of competence along the way and of course we were very thorough about keeping our security checks updated, but I have to tell you, Jas, I've got no vocational qualifications that would stand up in court. I didn't go to college either, but I expect you've checked me out?'

'My agent did, yes.'

'Then you'll know our work was always low key. Looking after Ivy's granddaughter was a typical assignment.'

'That's exactly why I chose you. My girls don't want a heavy professional presence. Obviously being who they are, they attract a certain amount of media attention, but I want to distance them from all that type of thing. I want them to grow up away from the glare of the spotlights. I want them to do normal things and in the absence of their mother they will need a responsible female they can rely on. Bella could be away all summer.

'At the moment she doesn't know exactly when she'll be coming home. That's why she is flying out to the Far East, to firm up on the details.' Jas hesitated. 'We're both agreed, we wanted someone who would be fun, someone who is street-wise, someone who wouldn't be afraid of getting down and dirty. Do you know what I mean?'

Andi nodded.

'At the same time we also need someone who can also be a bit . . . '

'Soft?' Andi provided the adjective he was looking for.

'That's it.' Jas agreed with an enthusiastic smile. 'You see, Holly's only seven. She's a sensitive child. She loves animals and she needs lots of reassurance.'

'And Misty?'

'She's sixteen.' Jas hesitated as if uncertain how to go on. 'She's a strong-willed girl, takes after me a bit in that respect, but underneath it all she's just a teenager.'

Andi had the feeling Misty could twist her father round her little finger. There was the faintest of challenges in Jas's jaw line as if he were daring Andi to confront him with her suspicions. He was definitely on the back foot and just an ordinary father when it came to defending his daughters, she thought as she lowered her eyes not wanting him to detect any indulgent amusement in her expression.

'So what you're saying is Misty doesn't want a nanny, but sometimes she's not as grown up as she thinks she is?'

'Agreed,' Jas said, enthusiastically. 'Do you think you can handle her?'

'I can remember all the angst of being sixteen,' Andi admitted. 'It was only eight years ago.'

'Misty doesn't need to know that and if you want to keep your authority, I suggest you don't tell her,' Jas advised Andi.

'Otherwise she'll try to run rings round me?'

'You wouldn't be the first,' Jas admitted with a rueful smile. 'You might have one or two differences of opinion with her to begin with, but hey, that's what life is all about, isn't it?'

'I suppose so. Where will the girls be sleeping?'

'There are two camper vans parked around the back of the building. They've got every facility you need. I thought you could have one and the girls could have the other, that way you can all have your independence and a little bit of privacy. Gradually you can move into the house, but at the moment that's just not possible. It isn't safe. Of course if there's anything else that you think I've forgotten let me know and I'll see what I can do about it. Any more questions?'

'You seem to have thought of everything,' Andi closed her notebook. 'That's me done.'

'There are a few pieces of paperwork I'll need you to sign. I'll get my agent to sort them out — no publicity or talking to the press, that sort of thing.'

'No problem.' Andi paused. 'You mentioned you had some questions for me?'

'Mmm.' Jas bit his lower lip. 'I don't know how you feel about this,' he began.

Andi's heartbeat quickened again.

'I've been approached to do a charity concert.'

'In London?'

Jas shook his head. 'No. Here, actually.'

'March Manor?' Andi repeated in amazement.

'Initially I turned it down, but the organisers were having difficulty finding anywhere else suitable and I began to realise it's not a bad idea. Midsummer is a lovely time of year. It's got a certain magic to it.'

Andi looked out of the kitchen window. What remained of the landscaped lawns was seriously overgrown. She'd been told there was a lake somewhere in the grounds too, but she had no idea where it was. In the old days there would have been a kitchen garden and she presumed an orchard, but that would have been a long time ago. The de Vigne family had done nothing to the property for years.

'The grounds are a wilderness,' she pointed out.

'Nothing a good contractor couldn't sort out and if we have the concert before we get to grips with the gardens it wouldn't matter too much what anyone did. I mean the fans could hardly damage a wilderness could they? What do you think?'

'You don't want me to organise it?' Andi was almost too horrified to ask.

'No,' Jas broke into a relaxed smile, 'I'm not suggesting anything like that, but if I go ahead with my plans it would mean more disruption for you.'

'In what way?'

'I don't know if you've ever had experience of a charity gig?'

'I've been to one or two parties in parks, but nothing on the scale of a Jas Summers charity fund raiser.'

Looking at Jas, Andi remembered to whom she was talking. His concerts raised millions for war-torn regions of the world and those ravaged by famine and drought.

'This would be low key, more a local event to introduce everyone to everyone else, if you see what I mean. Every year I choose a charity to sponsor, but I haven't had time this year. I wouldn't

47

be going global with this concert but I would like to dedicate it to my sister's memory. It's a personal thing so in many ways I don't want a lot of publicity.'

'Go on,' Andi urged him, excited by the thought.

'Low key or not, it will mean interviews, schedules which can be changed at a moment's notice, upset plans, hordes of visitors. I've got the infrastructure to deal with all that sort of thing, but you and the girls will be living in camper vans and you'll be right in the middle of the action.'

'Sounds fun,' Andi said.

'Do you really think so?' Jas raised his eyebrows.

'It will give your daughters something to do and take their minds off all the other upheaval going on in their lives.'

'I hadn't thought of it like that before,' Jas said. 'So are you up for it? Misty is of an age when unsuitable men may turn her head. I don't want her thinking she's in love or anything silly like that, and you'll need to keep an eye on Holly. She's so like her mother.' His eyes softened again. 'Bit of a dreamer and full of mischief and up to every trick in the book.'

'I think a concert is a wonderful idea,' Andi enthused, 'and I'm really looking forward to being a part of it.'

Her words were rewarded with a smile that set her heart racing. The phone began to ring on the wall and Andi watched Jas stand up and cross the kitchen to answer it.

'Darling, hello,' she heard him croon down the line. 'How are you? No, it's not the middle of the night here.' There was a smile in his voice as he asked, 'When will you get your head around the east to west time zones?' There was another pause before he said, 'I'm with Andi. She's going to look after the girls for us. What? No of course not,' there was amusement in his voice. 'Now you're being silly,' he said.

Andi busied herself collecting up

their mugs and plates. She didn't want to listen to Jas Summers laughing down the telephone line as he talked about her to his ex-wife.

She squirted a generous blob of washing up liquid onto the bowl full of assorted crockery and turning on the tap to drown out the sound of Jas's voice she started doing the dishes.

Getting To Know Jas

'We owe it to Andi to tell her, Harry.' Ivy looked up from loading the washing machine with Andi's laundry.

'Whatever you say, love,' Harry replied, picking up the newspaper and turning to the television page.

'I mean she was so good with our Kelly.'

Harry nodded, his mind on the evening's viewing. 'Yes,' he added scrutinising the schedule.

'Are you listening to me?' Ivy demanded as she closed the washing machine door, straightened up and flicked the switch to begin the washing cycle.

'We ought to tell Andi about the marriage break up,' Harry repeated with a sigh. 'I was listening, love. Whatever you do is all right with me.'

'And if Jas agrees, which I hope he

will, Kelly will be coming to stay here for the summer while our Sandra sorts herself out.'

Harry looked up from inspecting the television page. 'There isn't a problem with that is there? I mean I know we haven't spoken to Jas yet, but from what I've heard he likes family around him. I'm sure he'll agree won't he?'

Ivy screwed up her face in concern. 'I'm not sure. He's certain to ask about her and Kelly got in with an unruly lot last Christmas when Sandra and Dave were going through their bad patch. That may be so, but Kelly's the same age as that Misty that Jas is always talking about. The two girls are bound to pal up, aren't they?'

'I can't see anything wrong with that,' Harry said. 'They'll be company for each other.'

'Kelly's impressionable and nice as he is, I reckon Jas goes soft on that daughter of his. She's going to want a good time. You know what teenagers are like. Life at March Manor will be far too quiet for the likes of a girl who's grown up in America. She's the daughter of a famous pop star and a glamorous mother. They probably had swimming pools and parties all the time. She's going to find things here very dull.'

'I think you're worry about nothing, Ivy. Misty's young, she'll adapt. Besides, if Jas goes through with this charity concert he's talking about, they'll be plenty of activity. It will be up to us to make sure they don't sit around doing nothing all day. That way they won't have time to get up to mischief.'

'Yes, you're right there,' Ivy agreed, 'and Kelly trusts Andi so I'm sure if she's got any problems she'll go to her. I'd better have a word with Andi. She's a sensible girl. She'll keep an eye on things for us.'

'Is that fair? I mean, she'll have her hands full. There's the little one as well — Holly didn't Jas say she was called?'

'I don't think she'll be much trouble. She's only seven years old.' Ivy's weathered face creased into a smile. 'I've seen the pictures of her. She looks a little love. No, I'm sure they'll be no problem there. It's the older two I'm worried about.'

'Well, whatever you decide let me know,' Harry said as he ambled into the sitting room.

Ivy began to prepare supper. The break up of their daughter's marriage had come as a terrible shock to her and Harry.

'It's not working, Mum,' Sandra had explained. 'We've tried everything but we've decided this is as far as we can go. I know you'd made plans to move down here but, well, we're selling up. Dave's got a posting abroad, in Germany, and he's already moved out. I'm looking around for a job but there's not much for me here. I may have to move too.'

'What about Kelly?' Ivy gasped still reeling from the shock of Sandra's news.

'I haven't worked things out yet.'

Ivy's heart ached as she heard the tears in her daughter's voice. 'You will help out, Mum won't you?'

'Of course,' Ivy had heard herself say, wondering how on earth they would manage now they'd sold their bungalow.

When the job at March Manor had come up at short notice, Ivy had leapt at the chance to work with Jas Summers. Pop stars weren't exactly her scene but there was a cottage with the job, and what she didn't know about housework or Harry about gardening, wasn't worth knowing. Learning yesterday that he had also appointed Andi Cox to look after his daughters was the icing on the cake.

Ivy started peeling potatoes. She'd speak to Jas Summers about Kelly as soon as she could, perhaps later this evening, then she'd ring Sandra. The sooner they got things settled the better.

★ ★ ★

Andi inspected her camper van. Two identical vehicles were parked around the back of the house. They were brand new and painted with flowers, brightly coloured daisies. She smiled. Living aboard a psychedelic bus would certainly be a first, she thought. Someone had gone to a lot of trouble on her behalf and she appreciated the gesture.

Jas had handed her the spare set of keys and told her to make herself at home before he crammed his hard hat back on his head and ambled off to see how the workmen were progressing.

Space inside the bus was at a premium and all the basic necessities were provided. Jas told her if he could chivvy the workmen along, he would try and ensure that their bedrooms were finished first.

'That way you and the girls can all move back inside,' he explained.

'Where do you sleep?' Andi asked.

'I've got an old camp bed. I move it around depending on which bit of the house we're working on.' He delivered his answer with his usual charming smile. 'Takes me back to the early days when I didn't have any money and I used to bunk down for free in friends' flats.' He grimaced. 'Think my back was more up to the job in those days. I've grown soft or I'm getting old, probably a bit of both.'

If the article Andi had been reading was correct Jas was now thirty-six years old. He had been twenty and only married for a few months when Misty had been born. Bella had been two years older.

Jas was still whippet thin and despite his protestations Andi suspected he kept to a strict fitness regime.

Harry had left her two suitcases outside one of the camper vans and Andi lugged them inside. The bin liner full of washing was missing and Andi suspected Ivy had commandeered it. She blushed to think of how much dirty linen she had crammed into it. There hadn't been time to do a wash load before she'd left her flat and she had hoped to have access to a machine at March Manor. She hadn't counted on Ivy Preston being around and if there was one thing she loved above all else, that was looking after other people.

Andi gave a huge yawn. It had been a long day. She'd sort everything out in the morning.

Her mobile rang and snatching up her bag she saw to her delight the caller was Bill.

'Hi there.'

The sound of his voice always gave Andi a warm feeling inside.

'How're things?' she asked.

'I'm fine. I'm just checking up on you. Everything OK?'

'Absolutely. I haven't met the girls yet, but I'm going to collect them from the airport the day after tomorrow and hey, guess what?'

'What?' Bill asked.

'You remember Ivy and Harry Preston?'

'The couple with the granddaughter who was being bullied?'

'They're here too. It was lovely to see

them and we're going to catch up later. Ivy's already snaffled my dirty washing.'

'Jas is there too, is he?' Bill asked. 'What's he like?'

'He's very nice and not a bit like a superstar at all. He's actually working at the house, helping the men out.' Andi laughed. 'He was covered in dust from a fallen ceiling when I first met him. How's that for ordinary? I'm living in a camper van covered in painted daisies and there's another one for his daughters. Don't know what they're going to make of the accommodation arrangements. Bill?' she asked, as there was a pause down the other end of the line. 'Are you still there?'

'Yes. I'm still here. I was going to suggest you join me in New Zealand if you were having second thoughts about the job. My son's said you'll be very welcome if you'd like to come, but it doesn't sound as though his offer will be necessary now.'

Andi caught her breath. Bill had been like a father to her and she owed him so much. He'd come to her rescue when her life had been falling apart and without his help she didn't know what would have happened to her.

'Bill, I'm immensely touched but . . .'

'You'd like to take a rain-check on my offer? If I didn't know you better,' he teased her, 'I'd say you're in danger of falling in love with our superstar.'

'For heaven's sake,' Andi protested, sitting up straight on her bunk, all thoughts of going soft on Bill vanishing in an instant. 'What are you talking about now?'

'You're vulnerable. Tony Strong left you in a bad way.'

'Exactly, and after that experience, Bill, I can assure you it will be a very long time indeed before I let another man into my life. Now was there anything else?'

Bill's chuckle told her that she'd overdone the protestations. It would have been better not to react to his statement at all.

'You've got your laptop with you?' he asked.

'I never travel without it.'

'Good. I'll send you some photos as soon as I arrive in New Zealand. I'm flying out at the end of the week.'

Andi hadn't expected saying good-bye to Bill would hurt so much. She didn't know when she would see him again — if ever.

'I would come and see you off,' she began.

'That honour's already gone to my sister,' Bill replied, 'besides I expect by the end of the week you'll have your hands full dealing with teenage girls.'

'Bill,' Andi hesitated. She'd never been very good at this sort of thing. 'I . . . ' her voice almost gave out on her, 'thank you,' was all she could manage to say.

'Take care,' he said and rang off.

★ ★ ★

It was a few moments after Bill had rung off before Andi realised someone was tapping on the door. Scrubbing the

61

tears from her face with the back of her hand she went to answer it. Jas beamed up at her.

'How 'bout we christen your camper van, Daisy One, with a hot fish and chip supper straight out of warm newspaper?' He held up a greasy bundle. 'A perfect remedy for a broken heart,' he added.

Aware that her face was tear stained and probably very grubby, Andi managed a shaky smile.

'Come in.' It would be too embarrassing to explain that far from getting over a love affair, she had actually been saying goodbye to her ex-boss. 'I was about to open this,' she rummaged in her suitcase to find the bottle of wine Bill had presented her with as a leaving present.

'We'll use tooth mugs,' Jas said as he began unwrapping the newspaper parcels in the tiny galley area. 'Then you can tell me the story of your life. If we've time when you've finished, I'll tell you mine,' he offered, then added with a blinding smile, 'suitably edited for a lady's delicate ears.'

'There's nothing I'd like better,' Andi smiled back at him before going in search of the tooth mugs and hoping her delicate ears had not turned too delicate a shade of pink.

'Who Do You Think You Are?'

'Ms Andi Cox. Would Ms Andi Cox please report to the Club Lounge as soon as possible? Andi Cox, please.'

The tinny public address announcement reverberated around the arrivals concourse as Andi hurtled through the automatic doors. Her shirt was sticking to her back and she wished she hadn't bothered wearing a jacket. Unaccustomed to running in high-heeled shoes she could feel them rubbing blisters on her toes. So much for the professional image she had wanted to portray for her first meeting with Jas's daughters.

That morning things had gone from bad to worse, starting with the puncture down the lane leading away from March Manor. One of the security guards had tried to help her change the tyre by jacking the car up before he realised the spare was missing.

Andi had lost precious moments swapping vehicles, but that had only been the beginning of her nightmare journey to the airport.

After being caught in goodness knows how many sets of temporary traffic lights and road works, Andi had reached frustration overload when the police turned her away from joining the motorway advising her that due to a lorry overturning its load and blocking all four lanes, until they could clear up the mess, traffic was to be diverted down cutesy country lanes which would have looked charming on the front of a chocolate box, but not when you were battling against the clock, trying to get to the airport before the transatlantic flight from Los Angeles landed.

All of which made Andi well over an hour late arriving to meet her charges. What she would really have liked to do was make a swift visit to the ladies' room to repair her make-up and make some sense of her hair, but there wasn't time.

Bella had informed Jas over the telephone the night before that she only had an hour's window to hand over the girls and she expected Andi to be on time in order to minimise any hassle. Jas had assured Bella Andi would be punctual.

'The Club Lounge?' Andi puffed at the hostess on duty at the enquiry desk.

'Up the stairs and turn left.' She pointed the way with a perfectly manicured fingernail. Her smart appearance and pristine uniform made Andi feel even more of a scruff.

She crammed stray strands of hair back into her scrunch and hoping she would be admitted to the exclusive Club Lounge and not turned away because she looked like an undesirable vagrant. Another hostess was seated at a desk inputting a list of names into the computer. Her fingers tapped over the keys in a cool, composed manner.

'I'm here to,' Andi took a deep breath, her heart was hammering fit to burst, 'Andi Cox,' she gasped.

'You're very late,' the hostess said as she inspected her arrivals list. Her expression betrayed no sympathy.

'Yes, I know. The motorway was closed off due to an accident.'

Andi decided there was no need to go into the saga of the puncture, or the stop for petrol because the tank in the replacement car was almost on empty.

'Ms Ross was not best pleased to learn you hadn't arrived when she left her daughters airside in the care of one of our agents.'

'I'm sorry,' Andi repeated, 'but now I am here, can I see the girls?'

'May I see your identification and letter of authority please?'

She waited patiently while Andi searched frantically for Jas's paperwork. Her briefcase had shot into the footwell when she'd made an emergency stop to avoid a collision with a flock of sheep that had appeared from nowhere and blocked the country lane in front of her. The contents of her briefcase had spilled out and Andi had been forced to scoop them up in a hurried bundle as the sheep ambled along in front of her.

Along with having an almost empty petrol tank, the interior of the replacement vehicle had not been valeted and the floor space had born much evidence of muddy boots and half the forecourt of March Manor.

Andi's colour deepened as she handed over a crushed and stained envelope.

'Sorry,' she apologised again. 'Had a bit of an accident with my briefcase.'

The hostess wiped the envelope with a tissue before opening it very slowly and reading the contents equally as slowly. Andi bit down the urge to tell her to get a move on. The poor woman had probably had her ear bent by an angry Bella Ross, who Andi suspected, wouldn't be renowned for her patience.

'It says here you're a security guard?'

The grey eyes travelled up and down Andi's dishevelled appearance. Andi tucked more hair back in what had originally been a neat bun and tried to straighten her jacket.

'I'm also here to collect Jas Summers' daughters,' she said firmly.

She decided she had played this game long enough and now she was getting her breath back it was time to assert her authority.

'I take it my paperwork is in order?'

Her question received a brief nod in reply.

'Then I suggest you let me into the Club Lounge before I telephone Mr Summers to update him on the situation. He'll be most anxious to know his daughters have arrived safely.'

Moments later Andi was led into the cool exclusivity of the Club Lounge. The discreet murmur of hushed business conversations greeted her, along with the chink of coffee cups amid a gentle unhurried air of calm efficiency. The world of punctures and motorway nightmares seemed a million miles away.

'This way,' another hostess, the first to greet her with a friendly smile, guided Andi towards a far corner.

Shielded from the rest of the lounge by an impressive array of huge potted plants, Andi spotted her charges seated on plush leather seats, in the care of a comfortable looking middle-aged woman. She rose to greet Andi with a smile of relief.

'I thought you weren't coming,' she greeted her. 'I'm Mrs Jones and I was deputised in to look after the girls at short notice.'

Andi glanced over her shoulder to where Holly was colouring pictures in one of the books provided by the escort. She looked pale and there were dark circles of tiredness under her eyes. Misty was slouched in a far seat, arms crossed, glaring at the ceiling.

'I'm afraid I had to confiscate Misty's mobile,' Mrs Jones explained. 'She didn't seem to understand she's not allowed to use it in the terminal. Perhaps you'd better take charge of it and,' she added with a wry smile, 'the girls.'

'Is Bella Ross still airside?' Andi asked not expecting a positive reply.

''Fraid not. Her Hong Kong flight was on time and has just taken off. She left this for you.'

Andi blinked at the size of the file the escort handed over to her.

'Yes, I know,' Mrs Jones smiled, 'but she was most insistent I give it to you. I think it contains notes on their diets, their vitamins schedule and lifestyle guidance, that sort of thing.'

Before Andi could reply, she saw a movement out the corner of her eye as Misty slouched towards them. She was wearing an incredibly short skirt and more eye shadow than Andi thought was suitable for a girl of her age.

With her flawless skin and California tan she didn't need any make up, but Andi knew the girl would never listen to a suggestion of that nature from someone she probably saw as a dinosaur, and right now compared with this beautiful young girl, Andi felt like one.

'When are we leaving?' Misty's speech held the faintest of American accents.

'Hello. Misty, isn't it?' Andi asked smiling carefully. 'My name is Andi Cox.'

'I know who you are,' Misty dismissed her effort to introduce herself. 'Come on, Holly,' she called over to her sister. 'Time to split.'

The little girl looked up, beamed at Andi and dropping her colouring book on the floor ran towards them.

'Hello,' she lisped. 'I'm ever so tired. Where's Daddy?'

'I'll take you to him,' Andi promised, 'as soon as you pick up the book you dropped on the floor and thank this nice lady for looking after you while you were waiting for me to arrive.'

'You don't have to do any of that, Hol,' Misty butted in. 'She was only doing her job.'

Holly had already run back to retrieve her book off the floor.

'Can I keep it?' she asked Mrs Jones

with a pretty smile. 'I haven't finished colouring the last picture.'

'Of course you can,' Mrs Jones replied.

'And thank you for looking after us,' she added with a serious little frown.

Misty raised exasperated eyes to the ceiling and muttered something under her breath.

'Now it's your turn,' Andi insisted looking at her.

'What?' Misty's eyelashes fluttered in shock.

'Say thank you to Mrs Jones.'

Andi waited patiently as the older girl struggled to think of a reason not to do as she was told.

'Whatever,' she said eventually. 'Thank you so much for looking after us so nicely,' she parroted. 'My sister and I are really grateful that you took time out from your heavy schedule to care for us.'

'Now say it as though you mean it,' Andi's voice was firm. 'We're not leaving here until we do and may I remind you your sister is looking very tired.'

'Who do you think you are?' Misty demanded. 'You don't boss me around. You're only an employee. I could have you thrown out of your job tomorrow.'

'Don't, Misty.' Holly gave a little wail of distress. 'I want to see Daddy.' Her rosebud lips puckered. 'Don't be horrid to everybody. I don't like it.'

Misty hesitated for a fraction of a second before mumbling, 'Thank you, Mrs Jones. I hope we haven't caused you too much trouble.'

'That's all right, dear. It's been a pleasure.' Luckily Mrs Jones was a motherly sort who seemed to understand all about feminine teenage hormones. 'Now off you go with Miss Cox. Er, where did you park the car?' she asked Andi.

'In the multi story. Why?'

'The girls have got rather a lot of luggage, so unless you bought a pantechnicon with you, I don't think you'll get it all in.'

Misty surprised Andi by saying, 'That's all right, Mrs Jones, my father's driver can collect what we can't take with us. Mum always overpacks. I mean, like, poolside clothes for an English summer? Get real. We'll probably need boots and wax jackets. Do you think we can go shopping in town next week, Andi?'

Marvelling at this change in the girl, Andi found herself agreeing to a shopping trip and after a porter had been arranged to escort them to the car with the luggage they decided to take with them, they were soon bowling along the country lanes, back towards Old Haven.

'Everywhere is so small,' Misty complained as she looked out of the car window.

Andi frowned, wondering if she had imagined the faint wobble in the girl's voice.

'Don't you like it?' Andi asked.

'It's OK, I suppose. Just different.'

Andi glanced in the rearview mirror.

75

Holly had fallen asleep the moment she scrambled in the car. Her little pink hat had slipped sideways off her blonde curls and Andi felt a maternal urge to straighten it and tuck her hair behind her ears.

Her heart had warmed fractionally towards Misty too who for all her assumed street cred would appear to have a soft spot for her adopted baby sister.

Andi had to agree Holly's blue eyes would melt the hardest heart and it was a relief to know that she wouldn't have the problem of worrying about any sibling rivalry between the two girls.

'So how did you get this job?' Misty demanded.

'Your father wanted you to have some female security while your mother is away.'

'You're not like any other security guard I know,' Misty said.

'Don't you want one?' Andi asked, not sure if Misty's comment was a criticism or a compliment.

'It's cool,' Misty shrugged as if the

matter was of no importance to her. 'I do pretty much as I like anyway so it won't make any difference to me if we have one or not.'

'I don't think your father sees it quite like that and I've a few views of my own on the subject.'

'You?' Misty repeated in amazement. 'What sort of views.'

'If I'm to be responsible for your safety while you're in my care I set the grounds rules so you'll do as I say.'

'Excuse me, did you take your dragon pills for breakfast?' Misty demanded a ghost of a smile touching her lips. For a fleeting second her expression reminded Andi of Jas's.

'Just so as we know where we stand,' Andi said. 'You break the rules and you're grounded. Understood?'

'Yes, Ma'am,' Misty acknowledged with a playful salute.

Her mobile phone bleeped into life before Andi could respond, leaving Misty to spend the rest of the journey back to March Manor texting her friends.

A Growing Closeness For Andi And Jas

'How are you getting on with the girls?' Ivy asked as she poured out the coffee.

Andi nibbled on one of Ivy's home-baked biscuits wondering how much she should tell her. Much as she liked her, she could be a bit of a gossip and Andi didn't want word getting back to Jas that she had been talking about his daughters behind their backs.

The truth was she'd had one or two robust personality clashes with Misty. The shopping trip had been a nightmare with Misty playing up and Holly still tired from the flight. It had been a very dishevelled party who had finally made their way back to March Manor.

So far Jas had sided with Andi, but she suspected it only needed Bella to get wind of his support for an employee and the situation could change in an instant. From casual remarks Misty had made, Andi gathered her mother had a controlling personality.

'Kelly's changed so much I hardly recognised her.' Andi evaded a direct reply about Jas's daughters.

The girl had arrived a few days after Misty. She had shot up in height and now towered over Andi. She also appeared to think it deeply uncool to be friends with Andi and they'd exchanged no more than half-a-dozen words.

A shadow crossed Ivy's face. 'I hope she and Misty don't get up to too much mischief. I promised Jas that Kelly would be no trouble but girls change so much at that age it's difficult to keep up with them.'

'Where are they now?' Andi asked.

'They said they were going to help the volunteer party clear some ground over by the lake. Apparently Jas wants to set up the temporary stage for the concert under the trees, but it's been a long time since anyone's attended to the brambles and it's very overgrown. They've got diggers and heaven knows what else down there.'

'This volunteer party . . . ' Andi began.

'A lot of young lads from the village,' Ivy confirmed with pursed lips. 'That's why I had Harry go over there with them. He's a useful pair of hands on him and the girls won't come to any harm with him around. Jas is somewhere over there too. I believe he is keeping an eye on things as well.'

Andi allowed herself to relax a little. So far Kelly and Misty had done nothing more worrisome than disappear for several hours one afternoon without telling anyone where they were going. Andi had finally found them trying to light a fire in the woods on which to cook their sausages. They were desperately hungry, but too proud to come back and ask for help.

Jas had roared with laughter when Andi had told him what they had been up to.

'For goodness sake don't tell Bella,' he insisted. 'The girls are only supposed to eat organically grown products. If she found out about this she'd have the food police down on our heads before you could say fried sausages. Send 'em on down to the kitchen, I'll do them a proper Irish breakfast.'

'But it's four o'clock in the afternoon,' Andi protested.

'It's served all day where I come from,' Jas insisted with his trademark smile.

★ ★ ★

'I had heard,' Ivy began, 'that the village boys want to throw an impromptu party later on tonight. They were asking Jas if they could take some music and the barbecue down there. I think I'll go down and supervise the catering.'

'Good idea,' Andi agreed. 'I'll have to stay up here and look after Holly. She's far too young for that sort of party.'

'I hope she's not too lonely,' Ivy said,

'I mean Misty and Kelly have got each other. She could do with a little friend too.'

'Holly is animal mad. She says she wants to be a vet when she grows up. She's already got a baby rabbit to look after and she's adopted a stray kitten and Jas had promised her a pony as well.'

'You'd hardly believe they were sisters, would you?' Ivy said with an indulgent smile.

Andi was unsure exactly how much of the family history Ivy knew so she contented herself with an acknowledging smile.

'By the way,' Ivy began, 'I've been meaning to have a quiet word with you about Sandra. You remember my daughter? You must be wondering why our plans changed at such short notice.'

'You don't have to tell me anything, Ivy.'

'I want to,' she insisted. 'As you know we were all set to move down to the West Country to be near her. We'd had a good offer for the bungalow, so we sold up and were ready to go. Then a week before we were due to leave we got a phone call out of the blue from Sandra saying she and her husband were separating. I'd known for some time that things weren't too good between them, but I'd no idea they were so bad.'

'It must have been a shock for you,' Andi sympathised.

'Naturally my first thought was for Kelly.'

'I can imagine.'

'You remember what happened the last time there was trouble?'

Andi nodded.

'She's a lot older this time round and I thought without her father's influence to steady her and Sandra out all day, she might drift back into her old ways what with the school holidays coming up. So I suggested to Jas that as she'd already broken up from school would he mind if she came here for part of the holidays? He was fine about it, especially when he learned she was about the same age as Misty. My only problem is I don't want Kelly causing any upset.'

'She won't,' Andi assured her. 'Kelly learned her lesson last time.'

She had grown up a lot since Andi had last seen her. Five years ago she had been a slightly overweight nervous girl, the victim of some vicious school bullying. Now she was a slender teenager, admittedly with a bit of an attitude problem, but nothing a summer's fresh air and sunshine wouldn't sort out. Andi was convinced of that.

'Supposing she finds herself a boyfriend from among the village lads?' Ivy asked with a frown.

'It's all part of the process of growing up, Ivy. Don't worry.'

'I just don't want to cause more hassle for Jas. I think he's going to have his hands full. One problem after another it's been with the house, and what this concert as well, the poor man's got more than enough to contend with.'

For all his previous bad boy behaviour, Andi felt Jas was a good male role model who took his duties as a father seriously. He wasn't above helping Holly feed the rabbit and he was forever making cups of tea for everyone and helping out with odd jobs around the house when he had a spare moment.

'I'm convinced he won't let any harm come to any of the girls while they're in his care and that includes Kelly.'

'Well, if you say so. Harry and I always had the greatest respect for you and Bill. How is he by the way? Bill? Settled in?'

'I've got some photos on my laptop to show you when you've got a spare moment. He's settling in fine. He's even got himself a little job as a curator in a museum. When he's properly settled he's hoping to set up again in business.'

'Glad to hear it.' Ivy beamed. 'I do feel better for having got everything off my chest. Now, another cup of coffee?'

★   ★   ★

Andi strolled back to her camper van half an hour later to find Jas hovering outside.

'Where've you been?' he demanded.

'Having coffee with Ivy. I'm sorry if I'd known you wanted me I would have come back earlier.'

'I don't, not especially. So how are you settling in?' he asked as he followed her up the steps and into her van.

'Fine,' Andi replied.

'Misty?' he asked with a slightly raised eyebrow.

'We had a bit of a disagreement when we went shopping the other day.'

'I heard about it. Something to do with an unsuitable top was it?'

'What there was of it, yes,' Andi admitted. 'I know Misty is used to shopping for herself, Jas, but this was far too old for her and not really suitable for March Manor.'

'Understood.'

'I don't think I thanked you properly for sticking up for me,' Andi said. 'Misty did create a bit of a fuss in the shop when I wouldn't hand over her credit card.'

'That's why I'm glad you're here. I would probably have given in,' Jas smiled ruefully. 'I'm hopeless at scenes in shops. I hope Holly wasn't too upset by it all?'

'She'd bought herself a book on caring for rabbits so it all went over her head. She's the easiest child in the world to love, Jas. You should have seen the assistants making a fuss of her and it's not because she's your daughter. They didn't even know you're her father.'

'Holly is very like her mother. She was sensitive and a bit dreamy too. Everyone loved Brigid.' Jas's voice was slightly husky. 'When she died I thought my world had died with her. We were really close.'

A muscle twitched under his left eye. He cleared his throat. 'But she left us the best legacy of all in Holly.'

'What about Holly's father?' Andi asked carefully, not sure if she was reopening old wounds.

'What about him?' Jas looked uneasy.
'Doesn't he want to see her?'

'He's never played an active part in Holly's life. Holly knows she is adopted but as far as she is concerned, Bella and I are her parents and Misty is her sister. She's family anyway, so the exact situation makes very little difference.'

'Misty is very proud of Holly. You should hear her sticking up for her,' Andi said.

'Is that so?' Jas looked inordinately pleased.

'One of the lads was doing a bit of gentle teasing about Holly's rabbit. I tell you I almost cowered in the corner with him when Misty set about him. Poor lad slunk away with his tail between his legs. I think it'll be a long time before he teases Holly again.'

'So from what you say everyone seems to be getting along just fine?'

'Give or take a few squabbles. Yes.'

'And you? How are you settling in?' Jas asked settling down on one of the bunks. 'Like the van do you?'

'It's very cosy here,' Andi admitted.

'Good. It shouldn't be for that much longer. The builders are doing well with the bedrooms so hopefully you'll all be able to move into the house shortly.'

'I shall miss the morning birdsong. There's a small wren that's taken a fancy to me. He serenades me and Holly when we feed the rabbit his breakfast.'

'It is lovely here, isn't it?' Jas agreed. 'That's something I missed so much when I was away. In our business things can get a bit artificial and it's easy to lose touch with the real world, that's one of the reasons why I wanted to move back. I didn't want the girls growing up not appreciating the simple things of life.'

'Where is Holly, by the way?' Andi asked, 'I thought she was with you.'

'I've left her feeding lettuce to the rabbit. She says I can't do it properly and that I'm in the way.'

Andi gave him a sympathetic smile.

'She is very protective about her animals.'

'I know I encouraged my girls to speak the truth, but sometimes it's a bit much to take a lecture from someone so small on the etiquette of looking after a bunny rabbit.'

'I'll go and see how she's getting on later,' Andi said. 'You know if I didn't keep an eye on her, I don't think she'd come in for her tea. She loves it here.'

Jas stretched out his long jean clad legs and crossed his arms.

'Was there anything else?' Andi asked hoping Misty and Kelly wouldn't choose this moment to barge into Daisy One on the hunt for some refreshment.

Misty had begun to comment on the amount of time her father called in at the camper vans to see how they were getting on. She'd even made a veiled remark that she didn't think he was just checking up on his daughters either.

'There's a barbecue planned for tonight. Did you know?'

'Yes. Ivy was telling me about it.

She's already getting enough food out of the freezer to feed an army.'

'Want to go — as my partner?' Jas asked.

Andi choked down a sudden blockage in her throat. Whatever she had been expecting Jas to say, it hadn't been that. This was not the way things were supposed to be between Jas Summers and herself. Theirs was a professional relationship

After Andi's broken engagement to Tony Strong, her self-confidence had taken a serious nosedive and although Jas's invitation was only casual, Andi did not need potential complications of that nature in her life.

'Thank you,' she began, 'but I'm not going.'

'Why not? You get a night off every now and then don't you?'

'I've got to stay and look after Holly. She's too young to go and I'm not sure I'd want her to anyway. It would be very easy to lose track of her in the darkness. We'll stay here and watch one of her wildlife films.'

'I'm sure we could ask Ivy to keep an eye on her.'

'Ivy has already promised to do the barbecue. I don't want to pull her off it. She wants to make sure Kelly doesn't . . . ' Andi paused uncertain how to go on. She feared she might have already said too much, 'Stay out too late,' she finished lamely.

'Well, if I can't persuade you to join me, then I can't. Don't worry about the girls, I'll make sure nothing happens to Kelly or Misty.' Jas sprang to his feet. 'If you should change your mind you'll probably find me strumming a guitar under the trees. These days it only embarrasses my daughters if I try to dance.'

'I won't — change my mind,' Andi insisted.

'Fair enough. Want me to bring you up something from the barbecue later after Holly's tucked up in bed? We could have an intimate supper à deux? Chicken legs and chips in a camper van? It's all the rage I hear.'

'I've promised Holly baked beans on toast in the kitchen,' Andi replied. 'That and a banana are her absolutely most favourite things at the moment.'

Jas sighed and without warning tucked a stray strand of hair behind Andi's ear.

'You know,' he said as the tip of Andi's ear burned under the touch of his fingers. 'You're a difficult girl to date.'

Andi flinched away from his touch. 'At the risk of losing my job . . . ' she began.

'You're going to tell me to back off?'

'Yes,' she admitted.

'Why?'

'For one reason, there are the girls to consider.'

'You're using them as an excuse, aren't you? What's the real reason you're turning down me down?' Jas asked. 'By the way, it was only an invite to share a sausage or two under the stars, nothing more.'

'Jas, I'm not looking for a relationship, however casual, and if I was,' Andi warmed to her theme, 'it wouldn't be here or now,' she hesitated then added hoping her words wouldn't hurt him too much, 'or with you.'

Jas raised his eyebrows in surprise. 'I see my daughters have been giving you lessons in plain speaking.'

Jas's eyes were no longer honey soft. In the heightened atmosphere of the van they'd turned a deeper brown as if he were angry about something.

'I'm aware you're probably not used to being turned down,' Andi realised she had made a big mistake. For a while she had forgotten whom she was talking to.

Superstars had egos to match their status and Jas would be no different. Superstars did not take rejection lightly. 'If you're looking for a bit of company I'm sure one of the others would be pleased to accompany you to the barbecue.'

'There's no need to go on, Andi. I get the message. You're not interested.'

'Daddy,' Holly's voice broke the

tension between them.

'Hello, Princess.' Jas's expression changed instantly as Holly bounced into the van.

'You dropped your mobile phone in the grass by the rabbit hutch. It rang, so I answered it.'

Jas made a comical face at her. 'You haven't cancelled my next contract have you? That's my personal line you know. Only a very few people have the number.'

'Don't be silly, Daddy. It's Mummy for you. I told her you were in Daisy One talking to Andi.' Holly thrust the mobile at him. 'She wants to speak to you. Now, she said.'

Jas stood up slowly and took the phone from his daughter's outstretched hand.

'I told Mummy all about you,' Holly chattered on as Jas strolled out of the camper van to talk to Bella outside.

'Did you, darling?' Andi said distractedly noting the stiffness of Jas's body language as he spoke to his ex-wife.

'I said you were lovely and that we all liked you, even Daddy and that he was always sharing our supper and that he wanted to ask you to go to the barbecue with him. Mummy said to tell you she couldn't wait to meet you.'

Andi felt a chill of foreboding in her chest as she watched Jas finish his call, then without a backward glance stride off towards the house.

'Thank you for passing on the message, darling,' Andi said distractedly to Holly.

Her words, no matter how innocent, could already be causing trouble.

'Is it time for tea?' Holly asked. 'I'm ever so hungry. I think I missed lunch.'

A Threatening Letter
Causes Concern

'Where did it come from?' Andi asked, as she looked down at the crude words pasted on a sheet of grubby paper. A chill of fear seeped into her heart.

Ever since she had turned down Jas's invitation to the barbecue, communication between them had been strained and Andi hadn't seen so much of Jas over the past week. When she had received the message that he wanted to see her in the kitchen immediately she had assumed it was for an update on her progress with Misty.

The girl had taken to going out of an evening with Kelly and a bunch of boys from the village. When Jas had found out about it he had insisted on knowing exactly what was going on and who they were with.

The situation between them hadn't improved when Andi had argued their case trying to make Jas understand they were only doing what young girls did, then accused Jas of over-reaction when he had tried to insist Andi go with them.

'That's what I was hoping you could tell me.' The letter now shook in Jas's hands.

There was no trace of the easy going laid back Jas Summers. Today his face was a cold mask of suspicion as he confronted Andi.

'Why should I know where it came from?' She had difficulty controlling her breathing.

'You assured me you knew all about Misty's social life and vouched for the people she was mixing with. You told me they were a nice bunch of youngsters.'

'They are.'

'In that case, where does that leave you?'

'I beg your pardon?'

Jas flapped the piece of paper at her.

'Surely you don't suspect me of writing this rubbish?'

'It's your responsibility to make sure this sort of thing doesn't happen. I found it in Daisy Two on that table Holly's always using to do her drawings and it's lucky I did.' Jas was speaking in a controlled voice, as if he were having difficulty controlling his temper. 'You know how sensitive Holly is. Can you imagine what reading something like this would do to her?'

'I didn't put it there.' Andi was almost speechless with shock.

'Then who did?'

'I don't know.'

'You're in and out of their van all the time.'

'So are you,' Andi retaliated. 'So are half the people on site. We don't lock the doors during the day so anyone can go in. People come and go as they please, you know that. And what would be my motivation to do something like this? Holly's a sweet child, I wouldn't want to hurt a hair of her head and I'm trying to build up a sense of trust with Misty.'

'Yes. You're right. Sorry.' Jas removed his hard hat and ran his fingers through his hair. His shoulders sagged as he leaned forward and held his head in his hands. 'I don't know what got into me. I didn't mean to accuse you of anything. I just hoped you might have seen something.'

'Sit down,' Andi urged, 'and talk me through it.'

Jas sank into the kitchen chair.

'Have you had threats like this before?'

'From time to time, me that is, not the girls. I can take it in my stride. It's part of being in the public eye, I suppose. Cranks get a kick out of doing stupid things like this. Nothing has ever come of it, but I've always been careful to keep the girls away from that kind of thing. It's difficult to believe someone here would do such a stupid thing. I mean this is Old Haven. It's a sleepy village in the heart of the countryside.'

'It can't be someone on site,' Andi insisted. 'Everyone's made friends with everyone else and the guards on the gate vet all visitors.'

'Have you seen anyone suspicious lurking about the place?'

'No one.'

Andi picked up the crumpled piece of paper. She'd never seen a kidnap threat before. The words were cut from a newspaper and pasted onto a sheet of paper torn from an exercise book.

Andi frowned. 'It's a little unimaginative, isn't it — money or your life?'

'You're into the psychology of kidnappers, are you?' There was a sarcastic note in Jas's voice.

'I mean it doesn't really say anything does it?' Andi ignored his jibe. He was a father under stress and her professional instincts told her it would do the situation no good if she over-reacted.

'It says all I need to know.'

'No it doesn't. It doesn't indicate how much money they want, or whose life is under threat.' Andi turned it over searching for clues. 'It might be no more than a silly prank. Look, I'll try and make some unofficial enquiries if you like.'

'I'm not so sure it is a joke.'

Andi frowned trying to bank down her suspicion that Jas might know more about this threat than he was letting on.

'Then have you called the police?'

Jas shook his head.

'Why not?'

'I don't want them involved.'

'Until you do we are all under suspicion, Jas.'

'I've increased security at the gates. No one gets in or out without being thoroughly vetted and new passes are being issued.'

'What about the concert?' Andi asked. 'We can't go ahead with it if you're that worried?'

'Cancelling the concert is not an option.'

Andi's eyes widened in disbelief, 'You're not serious?'

'I've never been more serious in my life. I refuse to be held hostage to this sort of thing. Why should the charity lose out because some of oddball? Giving in would let them know they'd won.'

'But until you find out who sent it we'll be living in a fortress.'

Jas hesitated. 'Look, this is completely unofficial and you're the only person I'm telling, so if word leaks out I'll know who's responsible.'

'Go on,' Andi said slowly, keeping her voice carefully neutral. Jas was jumpy. She didn't want to spook him.

'One of the reasons I don't want to contact the police is because Bella's being difficult.'

'About what?' Andi asked.

'The arrangements here. She feels they are too casual.'

'In what way?'

'She likes things more regimented. Have you read through that file of instructions Mrs Jones gave to you at the airport?'

'I haven't really had time,' Andi admitted blushing.

The truth was she had been so busy she had forgotten all about it. It was somewhere on board Daisy One, but she wasn't sure where.

'It's very detailed and I would need to give it my full attention.' Andi hated to have to justify her omission. 'You're right. I should have read Bella's notes before now. I'm sorry. Have I placed you in an embarrassing situation?'

'No more than usual,' Jas sympathised, 'I'm not blaming you. Bella's fond of leaving notes about the place and I hardly read them either. Do you remember when Holly answered that phone call from Bella last week on the day of the barbecue?'

'Yes.'

'I think she gave her mother the impression that anything goes at March Manor. The children have never been allowed pets in case of germs and they've certainly never mixed with local people in the past as they do here.'

'But there's nothing wrong with any of that is there?'

'I agree with you, but Bella's hyper about hygiene and things like that. She also wants to know a lot more about Kelly, Ivy's granddaughter and . . . ' he hesitated, 'you . . . '

'I've nothing to hide. I can e-mail Ms Ross my resumé. Bill is in New Zealand now, but I'm sure he'd provide her with a reference. Do you want me to contact him?'

'Not at the moment,' Jas replied.

'I told you I didn't have any professional qualifications and you said that was fine. If you want to know about my personal background, my parents are divorced. I have one brother and a father who lives outside Canterbury. I'm sure he wouldn't mind you contacting him. The only other trauma in my life has been one broken engagement to a police officer. You could try running a computer check on me, but to save you the time I don't have a criminal record. Does that satisfy your requirements?'

Jas put out a hand as if to touch hers. Andi sat back in her chair anxious to avoid physical contact.

Holly was a chatterbox and she may have given her mother the wrong impression about the set up at March Manor. There was nothing between herself and Jas, but how could she convince his ex-wife of that? Andi was more than glad now she had turned down Jas's invitation to go with him to the barbecue.

She and Holly had sat in the garden playing with the rabbit and listening to the music coming from over the back then they'd both had an early night.

Misty had returned well after midnight, full of everything that had happened. Andi had only given half an ear to her excited account of the boys she and Kelly had danced with. It had all sounded very innocent, but Andi had been in a deep sleep before Misty had banged on her door and bounded into the van and hadn't given the girl her full attention.

'You're not listening,' Misty had complained as Andi tried unsuccessfully to stifle a huge yawn behind the back of her hand. 'I'm going to telephone Mum in Hong Kong; at least she'll be awake.'

Andi was more than aware that teenage girls could ramp up the action. Misty had probably given Bella a hugely exaggerated account of what had gone on at the barbecue and it was no wonder Bella was over-reacting to the security situation at March Manor.

'There's something I ought to tell you,' Jas said. 'Bella told me she's drawn up a short list of suitable candidates she would like to interview for the position of looking after the girls for the rest of the summer holiday,' he informed Andi.

'You mean I'm being fired?'

'That's not what I meant at all.' Jas sighed. 'Things were going so well. I thought moving back home we'd manage to put the past behind us.'

'The past?'

'Did Bill Branch tell you why our last nanny left?'

'I think he said something about her getting married.'

'She was expecting a baby.'

'I see. Well, anyway, Bill also told me Ms Ross, wanted to be in on interviewing the new candidates and that's why you needed me to look after your daughters until further arrangements could be made.'

'That's only half the story.' Jas took a deep breath. 'Bella more or less accused me of having an affair with our nanny.'

'What?'

'Keep your voice down,' Jas hissed looking over his shoulder. 'Walls have ears and you might have noticed there's a serious lack of doors in the house.'

Over the past week, several doors and walls had had to be demolished and the kitchen was the only place Jas and Andi could be sure of any privacy, and even then the privacy was unreliable.

'So you can see we have a situation on our hands.'

'There wasn't anything between you and the nanny, was there?' Andi asked hesitantly, remembering several intimate suppers she and Jas had shared in Daisy One. Perhaps he'd made a habit of sharing his suppers with her predecessor.

'She was a happily married woman, so the answer to your question is no. Bella gets these suspicions sometimes. I can't blame her. Our business isn't the most reliable of professions and every day I hear gossip. It's not my scene, but there were always fans hanging around the gates of our house in California. I used to speak to them and sign autographs, but nothing more,' Jas shrugged, 'that sort of thing can be tiresome to wives. Poor Bella simply had enough.'

'I can understand,' Andi agreed, feeling a pang of sympathy for Jas's glamorous ex-wife. She knew what it was like to discover the love of your life was unfaithful to you, not that there was any indication that Jas had in any way been unfaithful to Bella.

'Are you expecting a visit from Ms Ross? I thought your wife, your ex-wife I mean, was going to be away all summer?'

'So did I,' Jas agreed with a terse nod of his head. 'But it's not unknown for Bella to change her plans at short notice if it suits her. In the past I used to think it was her way of checking up on me.'

The more Andi began to hear about Bella Ross, the more she understood her motivation to pursue her own career, away from the trappings of a pop star's entourage. It would be very easy to lose your own identity.

'So you can see, if Bella got wind of this,' Jas tapped the note with his forefinger, 'she would be on the first plane back home.'

'What are we going to do? I mean if there really is a serious threat to Misty and Holly's safety, shouldn't she be told?'

'I'm relying on you, Andi, to keep an

extra vigilant eye on the girls.'

'I do that already, but I can't follow their every move. Misty's a bright girl. She'd notice something was up immediately, besides, she needs her space. She doesn't want me crowding her all the time.'

'What do you know about Kelly?' Jas asked.

'Ivy's granddaughter?'

'There was some bother with her a while ago wasn't there?'

'Yes, but nothing serious. She used to hang around with a bit of a bad crowd but luckily she outgrew them. She doesn't mix with them any more. I think she's trying for a place at the Art and Design College in the autumn.'

'What does Kelly do for money?'

'I'm sure Ivy would lend her any funds she needed.'

'Ivy's idea of a loan may not be quite so generous as Kelly's.'

'You're not suggesting Kelly left this letter in Daisy Two are you?'

'Do you think it would be the sort of

thing she would do?'

'No way. Kelly and Misty are friends and if they want money for any reason Misty only has to come to you.'

'Misty has a more than generous allowance. She doesn't need any money. I shouldn't imagine Kelly is in the same position.'

'Maybe not.' Andi was beginning to grow impatient with Jas's accusations. She'd made every allowance for his behaviour, but when he started accusing Ivy's granddaughter, enough was enough.

'Kelly isn't the pampered daughter of a pop star, but that doesn't mean to say she's a blackmailer. She hasn't had all Misty's advantages, and yes, she did go slightly off the rails a little while ago, but that's all behind her now. She loves it here. She wouldn't do anything to jeopardise her position.

'Ivy was telling me how happy she is and how she's hoping to persuade her mother to let her stay on with them. Like I said she wants to go to college to study design. She's got a real flair for that sort of thing and it certainly doesn't help having people like you making unfounded accusations about her. Perhaps you've forgotten how hard it is to grow up.'

There was a long silence before Jas said slowly, 'Perhaps I have.'

'I'm sorry,' Andi apologised. 'I shouldn't have spoken to you like that.'

'I'm glad you did. You were quite right to pull me up. Now can you keep as discreet an eye as possible on the girls for me? In case there is anything to this silly letter?'

'I'll do my best,' Andi replied, her heart sinking at the enormity of the task Jas had entrusted her with.

'Thank you.' He stood up. 'Best get on with the day.'

'How are the plans for the concert progressing?' Andi stood up beside him.

'Slowly, but we're getting there.' It was the old Jas who smiled at her now. 'The boys have cleared a substantial area of overgrowth down by the lake and the contractors reckon we're on course. There's a lot of work to do, but nothing they can't handle.'

'I was down in the village yesterday. I'm glad you're not thinking of cancelling. Everyone's very excited. I don't think they can quite believe your first performance back home will be in the sleepy backwater of Old Haven.'

'It'll break me in gently. It's been ages since I've done a live gig and it's something I've missed. I always feel as sick as a dog from nerves before I go on stage, but nothing beats the buzz of a live performance.'

'There you are,' Misty burst through the hole in the wall that used to be the door to the kitchen. 'I've been looking everywhere for you.'

Andi thrust the incriminating letter into the pocket of her jeans, an action not lost on Misty. A triumphant smile lit up her face.

'What's that you're trying to hide from me?' she asked. 'Is it a love letter?'

'No it isn't,' Andi snapped feeling her

114

cheeks burn under the scrutiny of Misty's perceptive eyes.

'Was there something?' Jas asked.

'What?' Misty looked at her father.

'Or are you only checking up on Andi and me?'

'Actually,' she thrust his mobile at him. 'You are wanted on the phone. You left it in the rabbit hutch again, didn't you? Poor old Mr Rabbit nearly jumped out of his skin when it vibrated under his feet. Mum got a bit of a shock too when I explained where I'd found it.' Misty giggled and for a moment looked like the fun-loving teenager she could be.

'Your mother's on the line?' Jas held out his hand.

Misty raised it to her ear. 'Think she's rung off. Don't s'pose it was important, but you really are going to have to take better care of your mobile, Dad.' She passed it over to her father. 'Anyone could have found it.'

'Did Bella leave a message or anything?'

'Nope.' Misty picked up a banana and began to unpeel it. 'I told her you were probably somewhere on site with Andi and she said she'd call back. See you later. Bye.'

With an airy wave of her hand, Misty sauntered out of the kitchen, leaving Andi feeling that yet again she had scored a black mark with Bella Ross.

Andi Visits Her Father

'Darling, how lovely to see you.' Daniel Cox's craggy face lit up at the sight of his daughter standing on the doorstep of his terraced cottage.

'Hi, Dad,' she kissed him on the cheek. 'Can I come in?'

'Of course.'

He held open the door and Andi padded down the corridor behind him. She loved his little cottage and every time she visited, she wished she hadn't left it so long since her last visit.

'I'm sorry,' she began as she followed her father into the book-strewn study.

'Move, Alfie.' He nudged the snoozing fox terrier away from the gas fire.

The day had turned unexpectedly chilly and the terrier opened a lazy eye at the sound of the commotion in the doorway then closed it again without moving a muscle.

'Darling, don't start by apologising.' Daniel turned round to face Andi. 'I'm your father. No apologies necessary. OK?'

'OK.' Andi hugged him again.

'Now, is this a long visit?' Daniel asked his daughter, his blue eyes taking in every detail of her strained face. 'You can stay all summer if you like. I won't mind.'

'It's just for the weekend if that's all right with you?'

'You know you don't have to ask.' His pale face lit up with pleasure. 'Let's have a cup of tea and catch up on all the gossip. I haven't got very much in the fridge for dinner I'm afraid, so how about I book us a table at Charley's?'

'Good idea. What is Charley's by the way?'

'It's a sort of barn-cum-restaurant and it's run by a friend of mine at the college, very 'in'. I've been spending quite a lot of my spare time there with, er, friends. I'm sure Charley will accommodate us at short notice.'

118

'Sounds great to me, Dad.' Andi put down her bag. 'Want me to put the kettle on while you make your telephone call?'

★ ★ ★

'I'm afraid I haven't heard of Jas Summers,' Daniel Cox said over tea as Andi tried to explain her new job to him.

'I didn't for a moment think you would have,' Andi replied with an indulgent smile. She looked around the room.

Every available surface was crammed with books of some description. Her father was an academic and never happier than when he was poring over a dusty document. His chosen field was the classics and it had been his idea to christen his daughter Andromeda. How he had been attracted to her social butterfly of a mother, Andi had never understood. The two were chalk and cheese and the marriage had been doomed almost before the ink had dried on the certificate.

'Is he very famous?'

'A bit, in his particular field of music,' Andi admitted.

'Then I expect your mother would have heard of him,' Daniel said.

'And I expect she'd be able to sing every word of *Song Of My Heart*.'

'What's that?' Daniel asked.

'It's his anthem you could say, a sort of rallying cry.'

'Wait a moment,' Andi's father frowned. 'That rings a bell. Some of my students mentioned something about a charity concert being held not far from here. I've got a flyer somewhere. Where on earth did I put it?' He began moving a few of his books around.

'Don't disturb anything, Dad,' Andi pleaded fearing the piles of books would topple over and create even more of a mess.

Alfie stirred by the fire and glared at them for disturbing his snooze.

'Perhaps you're right,' Daniel agreed,

beaming at his daughter from behind his bi-focals. 'So is he your new boyfriend? This Jas Summers? You know I never really took to that Tony Strong. He wasn't the man for you. Perhaps Jas Summers is?'

'Dad,' Andi raised her eyebrows. 'Haven't you been listening to a word I've said?' she complained. 'It's a professional relationship.'

'Yes, dear, I heard every word you said,' he replied mildly. 'This Jas's ex-wife has suddenly come home from somewhere abroad and you decided they needed time and space alone together without you hovering in the background, so you came to visit your old father for the first time in eighteen months.'

Andi flushed under the intensity of his gaze. As usual he had cut to the nub of the matter with minimum fuss.

'Is that how it is?' he asked, his blue eyes twinkling innocently.

'Yes, it is,' Andi conceded reluctantly. 'But I am not Jas Summers' girlfriend,' she insisted. 'I look after his two daughters.'

'What happened to Bill Branch?' Daniel asked.

'He sold up and moved to New Zealand.'

'Did he indeed?' Daniel polished his lenses with a spotted handkerchief. 'That's a shame. We had one or two good games of chess together in the past. I was wondering why he hadn't been in touch recently. I've been a bit busy what with one thing and another. I should have contacted him before now. So he's sold up has he?'

'Business was dropping off and he was finding it difficult to keep up with the ever increasing demands of the paperwork. Jackie always saw to that side of things. Anyway his son came up with an offer he couldn't refuse so . . .'

'He didn't,' Daniel finished Andi's sentence for her.

'That's right.'

'Good for him. And Bill arranged for you to work for this Jas Summers?'

Daniel perched his glasses back on the end of his nose.

'Tell me what you've been up to, Dad?' Andi asked, eager to steer the conversation away from Jas.

Her sudden decision to vacate March Manor for the weekend had been made after Bella's startling arrival when she and Holly had been busy shelling peas for lunch. Holly had raced off to find Misty and tell her the good news, leaving the two women face to face.

'Take as long as you like,' had been Bella's crisp reply when Andi suggested she make herself scarce for the weekend by visiting her father.

Bella's arrival had coincided with a professional crisis causing Jas to be called off site to settle a dispute regarding a member of his backing group who was being difficult over the date of the concert.

'Don Budge creating more trouble,' Jas had informed Andi. 'I'll be back as quick as I can. Can you look after things here in my absence?'

'No need for you to tell Jas where you've gone.' Bella insisted when Andi explained the reason for his absence. 'The girls and I need to catch up.'

Andi longed to tell Bella that despite her suspicions, she and Jas were not an item, but Bella looked in no mood to listen and Andi sensed her continued presence on site would only make things worse.

'You don't mind if I use the camper van in your absence? I'll need somewhere to sleep over.'

Andi flushed as Bella's eyes fell on the unopened file of personal details Mrs Jones had passed over to her at the airport.

'No. Fine. I'll pack a few things then I'll be gone.'

Al, the head security guard had made sure the pool car was clean and full of petrol and the tyres fully pumped up before she started out.

'The spare is in the back and it's serviceable, I checked. Don't want a repeat of last time I loaned you a car,'

Al said as he handed over the keys. 'Now are you sure you've got everything?'

'Thanks, Al.' Andi assured him she had. 'Sorry it was such short notice.'

'One thing I've learned working for Jas Summer is that everything's to be done at short notice.' He banged the roof with the flat of his hand 'Safe journey then. Where are you going?'

'My father lives in a small village on the edge of the North Downs outside Canterbury.'

'Very nice. Give my love to the cathedral,' he said as he waved her off.

And now two hours later, she was ensconced in her father's untidy cottage sharing a mug of tea with him and wondering why he was clearing his throat so noisily and wriggling uneasily in his seat. Andi looked hard at him. He was almost behaving like a schoolboy. If she hadn't known her father better, she would also have said he was blushing.

'Actually, er, Andi,' he began. 'There's something I've got to tell you.'

'Yes?' she leaned forward.

'It's about this dinner booking tonight.'

'What about it? Are they full? Can't they take us?'

'It's not that. No. I've,' Daniel continued to shift uncomfortably in his seat, 'made the reservation for three people.'

'That's all right,' Andi laughed, 'as long as you're not trying to pair me up with a spotty student, keen to expound his theory of ergonomics.'

'You know I'd never do a thing like that, Andi.' Her father looked shocked.

'So, who is this mystery third guest? Another lecturer?'

'Yes.'

'What's his name? Anyone I know?'

Daniel Cox screwed up his face as though he were sucking a particularly bitter lemon.

'Dad, are you all right?' Andi demanded growing concerned.

'It's not a he, it's a she, a female colleague. Her name's Hermione Richards and her field of expertise is Middle Eastern architecture.'

Her father's blue eyes widened as if expecting a challenge from his daughter.

'I see,' Andi said slowly, her heart sinking. She could imagine Ms Richards now — round rimmed spectacles, earnest faced and favouring knitted stockings that wrinkled around her ankles.

'I was going to tell you about her earlier but things have been a bit hectic here recently.'

'Dad,' Andi pointed out, 'you don't do hectic.'

'I do now.' If he hadn't been looking so serious, Andi would have laughed. 'Hermione's planned a holiday later in the summer. We want to visit the Arkeoloji Müzesi and the Blue Mosque and . . . '

'Hold on a minute, Dad,' Andi held up a hand. 'Did I hear you say you've planned a summer holiday with a female colleague?'

'Yes.'

'And you're going abroad?'

'Yes.'

Andi wanted to gape, but she knew it would upset her father and for all his absent-mindedness she loved him dearly. To the best of her knowledge, her father had been no further south than Brighton in his life, yet here he was talking about an exotic foreign holiday with a female called Hermione.

'Where exactly is this Arkeoloji thing?'

'Istanbul. It's a museum and it's got the most amazing display of sarcophagi and Hermione says the Blue Mosque is a sight not to be missed.'

'I'm sure it isn't,' Andi echoed faintly. 'Well, I'm very pleased for you and I hope you have a good time. Send me a post card.'

'There's something else,' Daniel added.

'What?' Andi queried suspiciously. She wasn't sure she was up to further revelation.

'Hermione and I are engaged.'

'Engaged?' Andi repeated wondering if she had heard her father correctly.

'To be married.'

'I thought that's what you said. Why?' she asked, hoping her father wasn't going to give the usual reason for a ceremony arranged at short notice.

To the best of Andi's knowledge her father had lived a comfortable bachelor existence in his cottage ever since the split with her mother. There had never been any mention of lady friends.

'Hermione doesn't think we should go away on holiday together without being married, so I agreed.'

'Do you love her?'

Andi felt foolish asking such an intimate question of her father.

'I think I do.'

If Andi hadn't known better, she would have said her father was in serious danger of looking soppy. He had a rapturous smile on his face.

'Everybody loves Hermione. She's wonderful. We've arranged a quiet ceremony for the end of the month. You will come won't you?'

'Love to, but does Mum know?' Andi asked.

'I thought you might like to tell her?' Daniel raised his eyebrows hopefully.

'No way.' Andi was firm on that one.

Andi's mother had been more than vocal on the break up of Andi's engagement, telling her daughter it had been her own fault for not making enough of herself. Andi didn't think she could be trusted to hold her tongue if her mother started making blunt comments about Daniel's new female companion.

'I thought you'd say that,' Daniel said gloomily.

Andi suddenly thought of her brother. 'What about Sam?'

'I haven't told him yet, no. In fact you're the first member of the family I have told. I know you'll like Hermione. She is so looking forward to meeting you.'

'Same goes here,' Andi admitted with feeling, wondering what she would do if she discovered she was about to inherit a stepmother younger than herself. 'I'd better start getting myself ready if I'm to make a good impression on your lady friend. Is this Charley's very dressy?' Andi asked.

'Good heavens, no.' Daniel looked horrified. 'It's full of students. An ex student of mine runs it as a matter of fact. He decided the classics weren't really his scene so he became a cook and he's a very good one too. Charley is actually Hermione's son.'

With her head still reeling from information overload, Andi and her father strolled down to the village an hour or so after they had finished their tea.

Andi hoped her father wasn't the victim of a manipulative female. She knew men of a certain age could be very vulnerable, and clever though her father was, he was seriously unworldly. If this Hermione put her mind to it, she could make mincemeat of Daniel Cox.

'It's not far to Charley's,' Daniel explained, 'and it's a nice evening for a walk, don't you think? Besides which Alfie could do with the exercise. He's done nothing but sleep all day.'

Many years ago, Andi's father had learned to drive, but after one or two arguments with roundabouts and traffic lights that would insist on changing colour and confusing him as he approached them, he had given up driving and opted instead for a bicycle before it was the carbon footprint friendly thing to do.

'Fine with me.' Andi slipped her hand through his and squeezed his fingers.

She and her father didn't get together very often, but when they did it was as though the years rolled away. After only an hour in his company, Andi began to feel better immediately. Thoughts of Jas and Bella and charity concerts and all the other problems that were currently crowding her life at March Manor evaporated, and if this Hermione had a grown-up son, perhaps things weren't as bad as she'd first feared.

All around them Andi could smell the country scents of a July evening, wild thyme mingled with damp blue-bells. An earlier shower had wetted the sun-baked ground and Andi inhaled the tang of moist earth and damp grass.

A clump of ox-eye daisies dripped gently onto the verge, their heads bent forward as if the weight of the rain had been too much for their frail strength.

Daniel stooped down and undid Alfie's leash. He was off chasing the scent of rabbits in seconds.

'He'll come to no harm,' Daniel assured Andi. 'He usually finds his own way to Charley's. When he's finished with the rabbits, he tracks the smells from the kitchen.'

'How long will you and Hermione be away for?' Andi asked as they strolled along.

'Six weeks. We're flying out then cruising back.'

'It sounds idyllic,' Andi said.

For a moment she envied her father his newfound happiness. There was a spring to his step and there was no denying he seemed a lot happier than when Andi had last seen him. Someone had cut his hair. He looked less wispy and he was wearing a new shirt and pressed chinos.

'By the way if you want to use the cottage at all while I'm away, please do. It might be useful for someone to keep an eye on things,' Daniel said.

'Thanks, Dad.'

Words hadn't been necessary between them for Daniel Cox to know his daughter might be in need of a bolthole at short notice.

'Here we are,' he said as they approached what looked like a brightly lit shed. 'Don't let the décor fool you,' Daniel said, 'Charley will cook you the best meal of your life tonight.'

At that moment the door swung open and Andi found herself face to face with a rotund woman of indeterminate age, sporting a bouffant blonde hair do and wearing a caftan decorated with geometric purple shapes. Behind her stood a younger man, equally as rotund, wearing chef's whites and beaming from ear to ear. He bore a remarkable resemblance to the caftan-wearing blonde female.

'There you are, darling.' Andi looked over her shoulder, then realised the woman was talking to her. 'I've been dying to meet you. We are going to be such good friends. I feel it in my bones. Now come inside and let my gorgeous son fill you up with some decent food. Young girls never eat properly. Look at you. You're far too thin. She's a bag of bones, isn't she, Charley?'

Before Andi could register exactly what was going on she was enveloped in a bear hug that had her fighting for breath and begging to be released.

'There,' Hermione said when she'd finally finished squeezing all the breath out of Andi's lungs. 'Now we've all been introduced to each other, let's get on with the evening. Daniel, you naughty boy, you didn't tell me you had such a beautiful daughter.'

135

'Just go with the flow,' Charley winked at Andi after he'd kissed her on the cheek. 'I have done for years. It's the only way.'

A Warm Welcome Home For Andi

'Where the blazes have you been?' Jas was pacing up and down outside the security gates as Andi drove back to March Manor late on Tuesday evening, her head still reeling from the intensity of Hermione's welcome into the new extended family.

She appeared to possess an army of equally sociable relations who all wanted a piece of Andi. Her father's fiancée was one lady who knew how to party and no-one was allowed to escape her clutches.

Picnics and cocktails had been arranged at short notice. Then she and Andi had indulged in a retail therapy trip to Canterbury, where Hermione insisted on buying a whole new holiday wardrobe for her trip to Turkey.

She would have bought new clothes for Andi as well if Andi hadn't managed to restrain her on that one. Instead they'd contented themselves with lunch in a café overlooking the cathedral, a lunch that had somehow overlapped into an afternoon cream tea.

They'd dined out every evening along with a whole host of Hermione's friends, all keen to meet her fiancé's daughter.

'I've always wanted a daughter, dear,' Hermione had said, 'and I hope you'll let me be your honourary mother. I know your real mother lives in Scotland and I wouldn't dream of taking her place, but I'm always here for you and if you've got any problems I'm more than willing to listen.'

There was no rivalry from her son, Charley, either. He had been as delighted as his mother to meet her and Andi found herself wishing he was her real brother. She and Sam were not only separated by years, the only real thing they had in common were the same parents, but as her mother had always doted on Sam to Andi's detriment, they had never built up a close relationship.

Hermione had been incandescent with delight when she learned of Andi's association with Jas Summers and plied her with constant questions about the charity concert and whether or not Jas was as nice as his publicity would have the public believe.

'The guards said you were only going to be away for the weekend.' Jas was now all but snarling at Andi as she tried to wind down the window of her car to greet him.

She was beginning to regret telling Hermione that if anything Jas's publicity played down his niceness.

'I left a message on Bella's voice mail,' Andi protested.

'You're responsible to me or had you forgotten that little detail?'

'Of course I hadn't, but Bella said there was no need to tell you where I'd gone and for your information I only went to visit my father.'

They squared up to each other outside the security gates while the guard on duty pretended not to notice them as he busied himself writing up his notes inside his little box.

'You had no right to go off base without my permission.'

'Your wife said . . . '

'My ex-wife,' Jas corrected her.

'Bella said she would look after the children and as she had personal things to discuss with you it might be better if I made myself scarce. I did the decent thing and went away for the weekend.'

'It may have escaped your notice, but we are now almost into the small hours of Wednesday morning. I'd call that a pretty long weekend.'

'That's because Charley . . . '

'Who's Charley?' Jas demanded. His eyes strayed to the back seat of the car. 'And who's been presenting you with bouquets of flowers? You've been seeing a man haven't you?'

Andi's lower lip began to tremble

with amusement. There was absolutely none of the superstar about Jas now. He was acting like a suspicious boyfriend and she rather liked the idea that he had missed her.

'Can we all join in the joke?' Jas demanded as Andi lost the fight with her smile as it spread across her face. 'Have I said something funny?'

'If I didn't know you better, Jas Summers, I'd say you were jealous.'

'Now you're being ridiculous,' he responded with a mutinous thrust of his chin.

'It's you who's being ridiculous,' Andi insisted. 'If you must know the flowers are from my father's very charming lady friend. Look, I'm sorry I'm late back. I realise I over ran my time, but I haven't had one day off since I started working for you and Bella did say I could take as long as I liked.'

'I would say you've more than made up for it, wouldn't you?'

'I really did only go and visit my

father, but he's gone and got himself engaged to a lovely lady, who incidentally is a fan of yours and is heartbroken that she won't be able to attend your concert. She's got a son called Charley who is equally as charming as she is and between them, they gave me a weekend to remember. There, that's all I've been up to.'

Jas blinked down at her and half moved towards her. If he had come any closer, Andi would have been forced to step back. As it was she could feel the car door handle digging into her flesh.

'Are the girls all right?' she asked when the silence between them became embarrassing.

'They're fine.'

'So no harm done?'

'Don't go away again without telling me.'

After all the shouting that had gone on between them, Jas's voice was now surprisingly soft.

'I won't,' Andi replied in almost as soft as voice.

Until she'd seen him pacing the perimeter of March Manor she hadn't realised quite how much she'd missed Jas, but Bella had first call on his time and Jas Summers had enough problems on his plate without Andi doing anything silly like allowing herself to grow close to him.

'I had a terrible weekend sorting out Don Budge. Then I get back to find you're not here. No-one knew where you'd gone. I thought you weren't coming back,' Jas said. 'Holly's distraught, even the rabbit's off his lettuce. Bella's upset just about everyone on site by insisting they go macrobiotic and Misty's got herself a boyfriend.'

'Where is Bella?' Andi demanded not relishing the idea of sharing Daisy One with Jas's ex-wife.

'She's gone,' Jas said. 'She had an urgent call from Hong Kong this afternoon so I drove her over to the airport. Ivy's been looking after the girls for me since I had no idea what you were up to. Bella's been very reticent on that one.'

'I'm sorry.'

Andi didn't know why she was apologising. Ivy was more than qualified to care for the girls and Jas must have known she hadn't disappeared for good.

'I've missed you,' Jas said so quietly that Andi had to lean forward to hear what he was saying. She could feel his breath fanning her cheek. 'Let's go and have a nightcap.'

'I ought to check up on the girls,' Andi insisted.

'I told you, Ivy's looking after them.'

Jas and Andi climbed back into the car and the guard activated the gates.

'What was all that about Misty and a boyfriend?' Andi asked as she released the handbrake.

'She and Kelly went out to a disco on Saturday night. It was a sixth form college do. One of the boys helping to clear the paddock had arranged it and they went along with Bella's blessing. To be honest Misty and Bella rub each other up the wrong way. Although she tries hard not to show it, Holly is Bella's favourite and Misty knows this. Anyway, to cut a long story short, Misty thinks she's in love.'

'Who with?'

'She won't say and she's sworn Kelly to silence. By the way Kelly's gone off to Germany to visit her father for a few days, which is just as well with all that's been going on here.'

'Did you tell Bella about that letter we found, the one we thought was a kidnap threat?' Andi asked.

Jas shook his head. 'I decided to play it down. I've had enough on my hands persuading Bella that we don't need a new carer for the girls.'

'Thank you,' Andi said, 'I thought my job was on the line.'

'Was that the real reason you took off?'

'I'm not totally sure. Bella can be very persuasive,' Andi admitted, 'and you did need time alone together.'

'We didn't get much of it. Misty played up. I think she was attention seeking. Then when she told Holly you weren't coming back, well,' Jas paused, 'you can imagine what it's been like.'

'Poor Holly.'

'There are times when I feel like throttling my older daughter.'

In the distance Andi could see the lights twinkling from Ivy's little cottage.

'So you sorted out Don Budge?'

'What do you know about him?' Jas's voice sounded extra sharp.

'Nothing. Bella said he was an old family friend? And wasn't there some confusion over the dates for the concert?'

She could feel Jas relax beside her and wondered why her question had triggered such a response.

'Yes. It was just Don being difficult. He's got a new girlfriend and she's planned this visit to Australia. He wants to pull out. I told him if that was how he felt then he should go. We had words.' Jas sighed. 'I'm always having words with Don. We go way back and as long as I can remember he's been difficult. We come from the same hometown and grew up together. I've always done my best by him, but I think he resented the fact that my career took off and his didn't.'

The twinkling lights of Ivy's cottage turned into a huge shaft of electric light as the door flew open and various shadows burst out onto the patch of lawn outside.

'Daddy,' Andi heard Holly's high treble, 'did you find her?'

Andi slammed on the brakes as the smallest shadow ran towards the car.

'Hello, darling.' Andi was out of the driver's seat in a flash. 'Did you miss me?'

She held out her arms.

'Andi.' Holly hurled herself into them. 'You left without saying good bye. I had to finish shelling the peas all by myself, then Misty said you weren't coming back.'

Over her little head Andi's eyes met those of Misty's. She smiled brightly at the older girl. She knew all about being sidelined in favour of the favourite. Her own mother had made no secret of her favouritism for Sam.

'Hello, Misty,' she said. 'Are you going to give me a hug too? Or are you too old for that sort of thing now you've got a boyfriend?'

Misty ambled towards her then broke into a rather undignified run.

'Sorry,' she mumbled into Andi's hair. 'I thought you'd deserted us, like Mum.'

'For goodness sake,' Ivy was now tutting around them, 'all this fuss because Andi took the weekend off. She's entitled to time away from you lot, you know. Hello, dear.' Ivy found a bit of spare space and kissed her on the cheek. 'Did you have a good weekend? Lovely to have you back. Now if it's not too much trouble, perhaps you'd take the girls back to the house so Harry and me can get some rest?'

'I'll drive the car round the back,' Jas murmured in her ear, 'if you'll get Holly to bed? Then come over to the house for that nightcap? Nothing stronger than hot chocolate, I promise.'

The look he gave her was as warm as hot chocolate and Andi was glad his daughters couldn't see the flush rising up her neck.

'That would be lovely,' she said in a husky voice.

'Come on, Andi,' Holly pulled at her hand, 'Daddy can wait, we've got to feed Mr Rabbit some lettuce first. He's been worried about you too.'

'I'm Not Telling You Anything'

'It is good to see you back.' Ivy greeted Andi the next morning. 'You've no idea how disruptive that Bella Ross can be. I mean I hate to speak ill of someone behind their back, but honestly she pushed me to the end of my tether on more than one occasion.'

Ivy's face was unusually pink with annoyance.

'I'm sorry to hear that.'

Andi was careful to keep her voice neutral. Like Ivy she didn't really want to gossip about Bella and she didn't want word getting back to Jas that she and Ivy had been dishing the dirt on his ex-wife.

Jas had explained over their nightcap that Bella's abrupt departure meant they had made no real plans regarding the appointment of a new carer for their daughters. As Bella was due to be away for at least two weeks, he had argued the case for Andi and suggested the situation continue as before. Bella had reluctantly been forced to agree. All of which was unsettling for Andi.

'Ms Ross inferred that my cooking wasn't macrobiotic? Is that the right word?' Ivy's face was screwed up in confusion.

Andi hid a smile. Ivy's cooking was of the wonderful traditional variety, lashings of delicious gravy on meat pies and creamy custard, poured over fresh fruit crumbles. Every mouthful was much enjoyed by the entire workforce at March Manor.

'What's that all about then?' Ivy demanded.

'It's a form of cooking which only uses ingredients that have been grown in a chemical-free environment.'

From the look on Ivy's face, Andi might just as well have been speaking in a foreign language.

'Well I don't know anything about

chemicals, I always use fresh ingredients from Harry's allotment and I've
had no complaints about my cooking
from anyone so I intend to carry on as
I've always done.'

Ivy delivered this robust statement
with a brisk nod of her head and a
crossing of her arms.

'What I really came about,' Andi
began, anxious to move the conversation away from Bella Ross, 'was to ask
you if Kelly said anything about Misty's
boyfriend before she left.'

Ivy uncrossed her arms and sipped
some tea. 'No, she didn't. There were
plenty of young lads around on the day
of the barbecue, but Jas and I kept an
eye on things and none of them seemed
to be getting over-friendly with the
girls. There was a bit of dancing, that
sort of thing, but nothing special that I
could see.'

'What about this disco the girls went
to?'

'I don't know anything about that.
They weren't back late because Kelly

had to fly out the next day. She's gone to visit her father for a week or two. I did tell you he was working abroad?'

'Yes.'

'He's in Germany and he's got some sort of contact in the art and design world. Kelly's really keen on doing a college course and leapt at the chance to meet this Frau Schmidt, I think she said she was called. You wouldn't believe the change in that girl.

'She was so excited about seeing her father again. You know I never thought I'd say this, but it might not have been such a bad thing for her parents to split up. Everyone gets on so much better now. Sandra's found herself a nice little flat and she's got a job and a car. Kelly's hoping to go to college and her father's helping her all he can.'

'I'm pleased to hear it.' Andi glanced at her watch. 'I'd better get back to the girls before they send out a search party.'

'Drop in next time you're passing,' Ivy urged her. 'It's nice to have someone normal to talk to.'

Andi walked thoughtfully away from Ivy's cottage. She hadn't suspected Kelly for a moment, but it was nice to know she couldn't possibly have had anything to do with the anonymous note Jas had found on board Daisy Two.

'Andi!' She looked up as she heard Holly calling her name. 'Over here.'

Misty was lounging against the gate watching Holly as she trotted around the little field on the back of her piebald pony. Andi waved back and went to stand beside Misty.

'Your father spoils Holly, doesn't he?'

The pony had been a gift from Jas to Holly as consolation for not having a friend to play with. Until last week Kelly and Misty had been constant companions and it now occurred to Andi that Misty might be lonely and resenting all the attention Holly was getting.

'Everybody spoils her,' Misty said

154

slowly. 'They always have done. I'm nobody.'

'That's not true,' Andi protested.

'You don't think so?'

The girl slouched off before Andi could remonstrate with her. Andi watched her slam the door of Daisy Two. The next moment loud music blared out the open window. Andi sighed. It now looked as though she had a new problem on her hands. She had intended asking Misty about her boyfriend and perhaps inviting him up for a barbecue so Jas could meet him on a casual basis, but from the mood the girl was in, it didn't look as though she would be getting any answers on that one.

Holly trotted the pony up to her.

'Isn't he lovely?' she jumped off. 'I'm going to call him Poppet.'

'I hope you're going to look after him properly,' Andi said as she patted the soft mane of pony hair.

'Of course. One of the workmen has cleaned out an old outhouse and we've converted it into a stable.' Holly's toothy smile was a picture of happiness. 'I've introduced Poppet to Mr Rabbit. Kitty's hidden herself away so they haven't met yet. Where's Misty gone?'

'She's playing some music.'

Holly pouted. 'She promised she'd stay and watch me.'

'The world doesn't revolve around you, Holly,' Andi stroked the anxious little face. 'Now why don't you go and settle Poppet into his nice new stable. Then you've got Mr Rabbit to feed and we ought to find Kitty. We don't want any harm to come to her do we?'

Holly was all smiles again. 'I like being busy and I like it here. It's much nicer than our other house in America. You won't go away again will you?'

'I've no plans to,' Andi said. 'Now off you go.'

'Are you going to watch Daddy rehearse?' Holly asked. 'He said he'd be down by the lake later.'

'Perhaps. Now don't wander off will you? I've got some work to do then what say we join Daddy?'

Holly skipped away leading Poppet carefully by his reins. Andi knew she really ought to make an attempt to read Bella's extensive file of notes.

She could still hear the bass of Misty's music thumping away and she knew Holly would never desert her animals, so for the moment she knew where everyone was.

Bella's file was comprehensive and extremely detailed. The children's weight and height were monitored on a monthly basis. Their diet was also itemised and there was a long list of do's and don'ts. Andi realised with a guilty start that Holly suffered from occasional allergic reactions and that was why Bella had insisted on the 'no pets' rule. Misty it seemed was only allowed to eat egg whites, not the yolk and neither of the girls were supposed to eat bread in case of wheat intolerance. Dairy was a no no as well.

Andi supposed it was too late to worry about things now. Holly adored toast coated with butter and lashings of

Ivy's famed strawberry jam and she seemed to have no allergies from working with her animals and last night when all the fuss had died down Misty had gate-crashed the kitchen and announced she was starving and proceeded to fry up two eggs and slap them on a piece of buttered bread.

Jas hadn't mentioned anything about forbidden foods and had followed his daughter's example and made himself a couple of slices of toast and coated them with a generous helping of Ivy's strawberry jam.

Andi gave up reading Bella's notes when she saw that neither girl was allowed to eat after six in the evening. As far as she could recall, they'd had supper together every night about half-past seven. Jas was always busy working during the day and seldom through before then and as he liked everyone to be present for family meals, to talk about what they had been up to, eating later had seemed the most sensible solution.

'I found Kitty, hiding in the meadow.'

Holly yanked open Daisy One's door. 'Can I have a biscuit, please? One of your nice chocolate ones.'

She had the lid off the cookie jar and was busy munching a chocolate finger before Andi could stop her. Sweet things were another forbidden food on Bella's list.

'Holly,' Andi began slowly, wondering how to phrase her question.

'Mmm?' she said through a mouthful of biscuit.

'Does Kitty's fur tickle your nose and make you itchy?'

'Course not.' Holly hiccupped with laughter then helped herself to another chocolate biscuit.

'I love Kitty.' She rammed the lid back on the cookie jar and clutching a handful of biscuits raced out the camper van. 'I'm off to feed Mr Rabbit.'

Picking up what remained of the biscuits, Andi sauntered casually round to Daisy Two. She knocked on the door.

'Go away,' Misty shouted back at her.

'I've brought you some chocolate

fingers before Holly eats them all,' Andi called round the door. 'Want some?'

Taking the lack of reply as an invitation to come in, Andi opened the door. Music was still blaring away in a far corner of the camper van. Misty was sprawled out on her bunk, surrounded by teen mags, make up and a box of tissues. It didn't take Andi long to work out she had been crying.

'These are really nice,' she smiled brightly. 'You're going to have to help me finish them.'

'I'm not hungry.'

'Couldn't you manage even one?'

Tears glistened on Misty's eyelashes and Andi's heart went out to the girl. For all her West Coast sophistication she was still only a sixteen-year-old girl going through all the traumas of growing up, not knowing what was happening in her world or how she was going to deal with life.

'Go on,' Andi urged her. 'Then what say we go and watch Jas rehearse? I've never seen your father in action.'

'I have,' Misty gulped, 'loads of times. Fans used to camp outside our house. It drove Mum mad.'

'I can imagine.' Andi pretended not to notice Misty help herself to a second biscuit. 'I'm glad they don't do it here.'

'That's because we live out in the middle of nowhere and there's nothing to do.'

'You could help with the concert.'

'Why?'

'I thought you'd like to be involved. I am.'

'You're only making yourself useful because you want to get into Dad's good books.'

'That's not true,' Andi protested.

'You were cosying up to him in the kitchen last night. I saw you.' Misty's voice was threatening more tears.

'Look, now Kelly's gone, why don't you ask a new friend to stay?' Andi tried a different tack. 'Holly said something about a boyfriend? I'm sure your dad wouldn't mind if he came to visit for the concert.'

'That's what this is all about, isn't it?

You want to find out about him don't you? Well, I'm not telling you anything.'

'Misty,' Andi began.

'I'd like you to leave. Now.'

'All right.' Andi stood up with a sigh. 'You know where we all are if you want to come and find us.'

Andi left the biscuit jar on the window ledge. Teenage moods were all very well, but she seemed to remember they made you very hungry.

As she jumped out of the camper van Misty turned up the volume of her stereo system.

'Misty's music is ever so noisy,' Holly complained as she trudged through the archway that led out to the courtyard where Poppet was stabled.

'She always plays it loudly when she's unhappy.'

'Do you know anything about her boyfriend, Holly?' Andi asked.

'She swore me to silence,' Holly lisped then gave a little giggle of excitement.

'I think you can tell me,' Andi coaxed.

'All right then, but you won't tell

anyone else will you?'

'What did she tell you about her boyfriend?'

'She said she was going to marry him.'

Andi felt as though she had been punched in the stomach.

'Was that all she said?'

'Think so. Then she swore me to secrecy. We always cross our chests and say hope to die when we do that. I told her my secret in exchange. Do you want to know what it is?'

'Not if it's an official secret.' Andi glanced back to Daisy Two. It was still rocking from the strength of Misty's music.

'I said I wanted you to marry Daddy. What's the matter, Andi?' Holly demanded. 'You're looking ever so cross. Don't you like my secret?'

Andi bit her lip. No wonder Misty was treating her as though she had the plague.

'I do, but I don't think you should tell it to anyone else,' she reassured the anxious child.

'Not even Mummy?'

'No, not Mummy.'

'All right. I won't.'

'Now,' Andi forced herself to smile. 'Shall we make up a picnic lunch and go and watch Daddy rehearse? That way we won't hear Misty's loud music.'

'Yay.' Holly danced a little jig. 'Come on, Andi. Race you.'

★　★　★

It was cool under the trees. Andi sipped lemonade as Holly ran around generally getting in the way.

Her pale little face had grown fresh air tanned over the past few weeks and she was putting on weight. She hardly looked the same child Andi had picked up at the airport.

'Hello, Don,' she waved across to a fair-haired man who was scowling at his guitar.

'Is that Don Budge?' Andi asked Holly.

'Yes. He's very nice. He's an old

friend of Daddy's and he's always telling me stories about when they were growing up together in Ireland and the naughty things they got up to at school.'

He didn't look like a troublemaker thought Andi sneaking a look at him from under her sun hat. Perhaps he was just jealous of Jas's success.

'Come to hear us murder a few songs?'

Andi jumped. She'd been so busy inspecting Don undercover she hadn't heard Jas approach.

'Is it allowed?' she asked.

'Be my guest,' he smiled down at her. 'You know you should wear yellow more often. It brings out the softness of your eyes.'

Behind her she heard Holly giggle. 'Daddy,' she chided him, 'can't you see? Andi's got a hole in her skirt.'

Andi crossed her legs quickly. She remembered now she'd caught the button on the door of the camper van as she yanked it open to see what Misty was up to. She looked at Jas with a resigned smile on her lips.

'Didn't notice. Sorry.'

'Why is it,' Jas complained, 'that every time I want to have a grown up conversation with you, one or the other of my daughters descends on us and brings us smartly down to earth?' He looked round. 'Where is Misty by the way?'

'Playing music — loudly,' Andi said.

'If you listen hard enough you might just hear it through the trees.'

Jas grimaced.

'Is anything wrong?' he asked.

'I think she's missing Kelly.'

'There's plenty to do down here.'

'She's not interested.'

'Ready, Jas?' One of the electricians called over. 'Need you on stage to test the acoustics.'

Jas waved back at him. 'Best go and do some work,' he said.

Moments later the afternoon air was filled with the strains of *Song Of My Heart*. Andi gulped. It was a song she had heard many times before, in many different places. She'd even sung it herself on student protests when she'd been a bit of a tearaway, before Bill had taken her under his wing.

But today it was different. Today she was sitting under a tree, watching sunlight dapple the grass, sipping lemonade and listening to Jas Summers singing it in person. She looked across to where he was standing in front of the microphone. Andi blinked and hoped her eyes were deceiving her.

'Daddy's looking at you,' Holly hissed in her ear. 'I think he's singing his song 'specially for you.'

Andi closed her eyes. She didn't know how it had happened or when. She had tried her hardest not to let it happen. Biting down a groan of frustration she realised now there was no danger of her falling in love with Jas. She was already in love with him.

A Panic Occurs At March Manor

'Come on, Holly.' Andi bagged up the remains of their picnic. She hadn't meant to stay so long, but the cool of the trees had alleviated the earlier heat of the day and she had needed some time out after her scene with Misty.

'Can't we stay a bit longer?' Holly pleaded.

'It's way past your tea time and we ought to go and see what Misty's up to.'

Andi glanced at her watch and saw to her amazement that over three hours had passed.

'Just five minutes more?' Holly pleaded.

'I can't leave you on your own, you know that.'

'Daddy's still here. Look.' Holly pointed a finger towards the stage.

Before Andi could stop her, Holly

had raced off in the direction of the knot of musicians and workmen huddled by the speakers. She saw Don turn round and smile at Holly and hold out a hand. He waved across to Andi who semaphored her intention of returning to the camper vans. He nodded his understanding and pointed to his girlfriend who was painting her nails as she sat on a sawn-off tree trunk.

'Want me to do yours, Holly?' she asked.

With a squeal of excitement Holly raced over.

Satisfied that Holly was in safe hands, Andi set off towards the camper vans. The walk back was uphill and before long Andi was panting from carrying the weight of the picnic basket by herself. On the way down one of the technicians had helped her.

Although the strength of the sun had abated its heat was still warm on her back and as Andi emerged from woods onto the front lawn she took a few moments out to admire the faded beauty of March Manor.

She was glad Jas had decided to only renovate the interior of the house. The outside walls could still hold their own and did not need any modernisation. The sun-baked stone basked in the afternoon sunshine and Andi imagined the generations of de Vignes who had enjoyed living here. Had they too held summer parties on the lawn? She was sure their events would have been gracious occasions accompanied by the elegant chink of bone china teacups.

Andi wondered what Victorian society would have made of a female security guard wearing a gappy yellow sundress and sandals and exposing an indelicate amount of skin that was turning dangerously tanned from over exposure to the summer sunshine. Her hair would make a decent bird's nest too. No doubt, Andi thought wryly, she would have been banished to the Colonies for life as far too bad an influence on the maidens of the house.

A slight breeze disturbed the overblown

cabbage roses and Andi closed her eyes as she inhaled their scent. At this moment March Manor was the most perfect place to be. She couldn't imagine ever leaving it.

Her own childhood had been disturbed, first by her parents' break up, and then by her mother's obvious favouritism for her brother, Sam. March Manor had been the first real place Andi wanted to call home. Quite how it had happened she didn't know. Perhaps it was because for the first time in her life she felt wanted. She was part of a proper family with Jas and his two daughters.

Over the short time she had been here they had somehow grown together. Of course there were petty squabbles and some days were better than others, but Andi imagined that was what family life was about. You shared the good times together and the bad and underneath all the emotion there was a sense of togetherness and love.

The tooting of a horn as one of the

security guards drove by drew Andi sharply back to the present reminding her she had better go and find Misty.

Leaving the picnic basket outside Daisy One, Andi crept towards Daisy Two. It was quiet inside now. Andi breathed a sigh of relief. At least the ear splitting music had ceased. She tapped on the camper door. There was no reply. She turned the handle and poked her head inside.

'Misty?' she called out.

Her enquiry met with silence.

'Are you there?'

Her bunk was still strewn with discarded make up, damp tissues and the magazines Misty had been reading. Andi bit her lip. It looked as though the girl had left in a hurry. She put a hand on the sound system. It was warm to the touch, so she hadn't been gone long. Andi rifled through the bits and pieces on the bed.

Her mobile phone was missing. At least she had had the sense to take it with her Andi thought as she swiftly dialled Misty's number stifling down a brief feeling of annoyance.

Perhaps Jas should enrol her for a summer school now as it looked as though Kelly would be away for a while. There must be something she was interested in. Ivy had mentioned art classes or perhaps she could take a course on sailing. That was always popular with the youngsters.

The number rang out but Misty did not pick up the call. Andi left a message on her voicemail then glanced at her watch. The guard had given her a friendly wave as he'd driven by the rose garden. That had been about half an hour earlier. She was sure if he'd had anything to report he would have stopped and told her. All the same, Andi decided to ask at the gate to see if by any chance anyone had seen Misty trying to sneak out. She was too young to drive, so she couldn't have taken any of the pool cars.

'Sorry, Andi, no, I haven't seen her.' Al was on gate duty.

'You don't know anything about a boyfriend do you? Someone from the sixth form college?'

'I heard a rumour but no-one's been through on my watch.'

'Will you keep a look out for me?' Andi asked.

'Sure thing. Don't worry,' he said. 'I've got teenagers myself. They are a law unto themselves. She's probably taken herself off somewhere for a bit of a cry. She'll come home when she's hungry.'

'I hope you're right,' Andi replied.

Misty knew she wasn't allowed in the main part of the house without an escort and Andi didn't think she would be silly enough to disobey the rules. That only left the grounds. They were extensive and Andi would need help if she were going to have to organise a search for the girl.

At least Misty had been nowhere near the lake, Andi thought with a sense of relief. To get there she would have had to pass the rehearsal stage and someone would have seen her.

Andi's sense of annoyance was developing into a growing unease. She didn't want to over react to something that was probably no more than a fit of pique, all the same, if she didn't find Misty soon, she would have to tell Jas that the girl was missing and that was a prospect she did not relish.

'No,' Ivy shook her head in reply to Andi's query, 'I haven't seen her all day. I'll get Harry to take a look round the house for you if you like. I'm sure there's nothing to worry about, but it pays to be careful. She might have fallen over in the kitchen or something.'

'Thanks, Ivy.' Andi felt immediately reassured. 'If you want me I'll be down by the lake.'

Several of the backing group were still strumming chords as Andi made her way back to the rehearsal area.

'What do you mean by leaving Holly with Don Budge?' Jas demanded as she approached them.

'Chill, Jas,' Don stepped in. 'Holly's fine with me and my girlfriend. They've been painting their nails.' He turned to Andi. 'Have you found Misty yet?'

'Found Misty? She's not missing is she?' Jas demanded.

'One of the gate guards said you were asking about her earlier?' Don said. 'Something about her going off with a boyfriend?'

'What exactly is going on?'

Jas's raised voice disturbed the rooks nesting in the trees above them. They flapped their wings and cawed in startled surprise.

'I was coming down to tell you,' Andi began wishing Don had let her tell Jas of her suspicions in her own words. 'Daisy Two is empty and Misty isn't answering her mobile phone. I was wondering if by any chance she had made her way down here.'

Don shook his head. 'I've been here all the time with Holly and the others. There's been no sign of her.'

'When did you last see her?' Jas demanded.

'Before we came down here to hear

you rehearse,' Andi replied. 'She was supposed to join us for a picnic but she never arrived.'

'And you didn't think to go looking for her earlier?'

'She said she wasn't hungry and wanted to listen to her music. She's been a bit out of sorts ever since Kelly went off to Germany. I thought the best thing to do was to leave her alone for a while. She was perfectly fine, just a little upset, that's all.'

'A little upset? What about?'

'I tried asking her if the rumours about her having a new boyfriend were true. I thought perhaps if they were we could arrange a barbecue or something to cheer her up and to introduce this boyfriend to everyone.'

'And?' Jas prompted.

'She wasn't interested,' Andi replied.

'Was that all?'

'Yes.'

Andi decided Jas didn't need to know everything that had gone on between her and Misty.

'What about Ivy? Has she seen Misty?'

'Harry's doing a search of the house now.'

'This boyfriend,' Jas's eyebrows were drawn together in a furious frown. 'What do we know about him?'

'Nothing much. I think he might be a pupil at the college.'

'I'm going down there.'

'It's after five. There won't be anyone there now.'

'Somebody must know something and I can't sit around doing nothing.'

Aware that their raised voices were now the centre of attention Andi tugged urgently at the sleeve of Jas's shirt.

'Can I have a brief word in private?' she asked quietly.

'What about?' Jas snapped.

Andi began walking away from the interested knot of onlookers. Jas followed her.

'If anything's happened to my daughter,' he began, 'I'm holding you solely responsible. How did she get entangled with this boy in the first place?'

'I don't know,' Andi retaliated, stung by the injustice of his accusation. 'Bella might know more about it. Why don't you try asking her? She was here at the time. I wasn't.'

'We should never have ignored that ransom note.'

'If you remember rightly we made a mutual decision not to do anything about it.'

'You said . . . '

'Hurling accusations at each other is getting us nowhere,' Andi hissed. 'I'm thinking more along the lines of supposing,' she paused, uncertain how to put her fears into words that wouldn't send Jas into orbit. 'Misty was feeling rather left out of things. Holly has her animals; you've got your concert and the house. I'm busy on various projects.'

'For heaven's sake, Andi, what are you trying to say?' Jas's face was a mask of barely controlled suspicion. 'Do you know something about where she's gone?'

'Supposing she's eloped?'

'Eloped? She's only sixteen,' he exploded.

'And old enough to get married.'

'You can't really think she'd do a stupid thing like that.'

'I don't know. I'm not sure.' Andi was reluctant to repeat the secret Misty had confided to Holly. There were enough false rumours flying around as it was.

'But if she hasn't gone off with her boyfriend, then where is she? The security guards haven't seen her but I'm sure she could find a way off the premises if she put her mind to it. I may be over reacting but if this boyfriend can drive they could be half way to Scotland.'

Jas whipped out the two-way radio he used to contact members of staff.

'I need transport,' he barked into the receiver. 'Any one of the cars will do. Bring it round the front. Now. If you're right,' he turned his attention back to Andi, 'I've got to find her before she does anything silly.'

'What do you want me to do?' Andi called after Jas as she watched him stride off through the trees.

'Stay with Holly and try not to lose sight of my other daughter.'

'I Want You Off
The Premises'

Andi trudged back to the camper vans with a despondent Holly in tow. 'Do you think it's my fault Misty has disappeared?' she asked.

'Of course not, darling,' Andi said, 'whatever gave you that idea?'

'I was showing off when I was riding Poppet and then Misty didn't wait until I'd finished.' Holly's lower lip trembled. 'I wanted her to help me feed Mr Rabbit. And I've got Kitty. She hasn't got anything. I was going to share my new nail varnish with her.'

Holly's words made Andi realise with a guilty start that everyone had rather overlooked Misty. Because she was a teenager, it didn't mean she didn't like being spoilt every now and then.

'I'm sure Misty's disappearance is

nothing to do with you, Holly and when we find her she'll tell you so herself. I'm sure she'll be delighted with the new nail varnish too.'

'Really?' Holly's face lit up.

'Really,' Andi smiled back at her. 'Why don't you go and put it on her shelf? Then how would you like to have tea with Ivy?'

'Please.' Holly clapped her hands in delight. 'I'm ever so hungry. Do you think she's got any of her special fruit cake?'

'Let's go and see.'

After Ivy has assured Andi that Holly would be safe with her and a hurried murmured exchange about Harry still being out looking for Misty, Andi decided she needed to change her torn dress and put on some jeans if she was going to join the search.

By now word had got round the site and everyone was out looking for Misty. All sorts of stories were being bandied around from kidnap threats to elopements. Andi had no idea how anyone had found out about either of these theories, but it seemed March Manor had an information technology program that would put any sophisticated computerised system to shame.

Andi tried not to think about the accusations Jas had hurled at her. They were cruel and unjust, but he was a father who was worried about his daughter and it was natural he would blame Andi.

After all Andi had been appointed as a security guard to his girls and now one of them had disappeared. Technically she supposed she was to blame for not keeping a better eye on Misty.

For the second time that afternoon Andi stood in the middle of the lawn and gazed up at the manor house. Where could Misty be? Where would she go? She wasn't in the house. Harry had searched it from top to bottom. All her usual haunts — the old vegetable garden, the lake and the paddock had also proved negative.

In order to leave the premises she

would have needed transport. March Manor was a mile or so from the village and Misty's favoured footwear was of the stiletto sandal variety, so walking to the village was out of the question.

Andi didn't dare dwell on the ransom note or what Bella Ross would say if she found out about it. They'd probably be talking lawsuits. After Andi's initial shock at reading the note had worn off, she had taken the line that it was only some sort of silly joke Misty and Kelly had thought up, perhaps when they were looking for thrills or enacting some sort of role-play. Until Kelly's departure for Germany the two girls had been inseparable. Half the time Andi had had no idea what they were up to.

She now realised she and Jas had been wrong not to take the threat more seriously. What if there was a stalker in the grounds, a stalker intent on making mischief?

Breathing deeply to control her shattered nerves and still unable to come up with any fresh ideas, Andi walked round the back of the house towards the camper vans. The novelty of living on board was beginning to pall and Andi found herself longing for a proper bedroom and space to spread out.

The picnic basket was still on the step where she had left it. Andi nudged it out of the way with her foot. She'd deal with rubbish later she decided, after she'd changed into her shirt and jeans. Some of the workmen had been talking about dragging the lake, but that would need specialist equipment and a team of experts.

Before they went down that route, Andi decided she would have one last search through the grounds. Maybe Misty had wandered off somewhere and had an accident — fallen down a rabbit hole perhaps and twisted her ankle. She could be lying on the ground, unable to move. If her phone had fallen out of her pocket when she fell, she may not be able to reach it to answer Andi's call.

As Andi climbed the steps to Daisy One she checked her mobile. In all the confusion she may have missed a call. There were no messages received.

She threw her bag down on the window ledge and yanked open a cupboard to find her jeans. Dragging a clean T shirt off her shelf she quickly got changed.

It was then she heard a noise behind her. She whirled round.

A bleary-eyed Misty was stretched out on her bunk, her face swollen from crying. She looked no older than Holly as she scrambled into a corner of the bunk and clutched at a stray blanket, cuddling it to her like a child.

'Misty!' Andi ran towards her and threw her arms around the girl. 'You're safe.' She cradled her head and kissed her damp hair. Her forehead felt warm and she was hiccupping with more tears as she tried to speak.

'Sorry,' she sobbed.

'There, there, it's all right,' Andi crooned. 'No-one's cross with you. We all missed you down by the rehearsal stage. We've been so worried about you. Where've you been?'

'I had a secret date, in the woods.'

A chill of fear entered Andi's heart. 'What happened?' she asked carefully.

'He said,' Misty gulped, 'he said,' she began again, 'that he liked Kelly not me and the only reason he pretended to like me was because I was Jas's daughter.'

Misty's slender body shook with another paroxysm of sobbing.

'I really liked him,' she wailed. 'Nobody likes me. Holly is Mum's favourite and yours, and Dad's so tied up with the concert he hasn't got time for anything else.'

'You silly thing,' Andi chided her gently, relief coursing through her body. Misty was safe. 'How could you ever think that?' Her heart was filled with sympathy for the girl.

Life was cruel at times and Misty had just had her first lesson in cruelty. She'd recover in time, but right now it must feel as if the bottom had dropped out of her world. 'You're my right-hand man.'

'I am?' The spiky eyelashes were tear laden and the eyelids swollen as Misty looked doubtfully at Andi.

'I couldn't look after Holly without your help,' Andi said, 'and as for your father not caring about you, do you know what he's done?'

'No.' Misty's eyes widened dramatically. 'What?'

'He's raced off down to the college threatening all sorts of retribution against this so called boyfriend of yours. Thank heavens we don't have a horse whip on the premises.'

The ghost of a smile tugged at the corners of Misty's mouth. 'That's the Irish in him coming out.'

'It's the father in him coming out. Fathers can be so embarrassing can't they?' Andi raised her eyes in a gesture of mock discomfort. 'And as for boys, who needs them?'

Tears welled up in Misty's eyes again. 'He said I was only a silly girl.'

'And you believed him?' Andi stroked

damp hair out of Misty's eyes. 'Well let me tell you, Ms Summers, you are one beautiful girl and if anyone says you are silly in my presence they'll have me to deal with. I may not be Irish like your father, but I've quite a temper on me when I'm roused. I've been on a self-defence course and you should see my kickboxing skills and I'd love to refresh them on a silly boy.'

'Cool,' Misty's voice was still a bit squeaky, but not quite so full of tears. 'You'd really do that for me?'

It was Andi who now found her eyes were beginning to water, from a combination of relief and a newfound empathy with Jas's elder daughter. She so knew what it was like to lose out in love.

'There's nothing I wouldn't do for my favourite girl,' she insisted.

'I haven't been awfully nice to you, have I?' Misty mumbled. 'I didn't mean those things I said to you earlier, about you being nice to Dad. I mean, I think he really likes you.'

'Tell you what,' Andi suggested, anxious to make sure Misty really was all right, 'why don't we get Doctor Suzie over from the house?'

'Why?'

'We want to make sure you won't be crying all night, don't we? Then after she's gone if you're up for it we could have a girls' night together? You could choose your favourite meal. Holly's got some new nail varnish we could snaffle. I'm sure she wouldn't mind. She wanted to share it with you. We could paint our nails and watch a film?'

'Only the two of us?'

'You're on. Then next week how about a proper shopping trip? I could take a whole day off and I'm sure Ivy wouldn't mind looking after Holly. I've heard there's a new beauty centre opened locally too. We could have a massage, get our hair done?'

'I need some make-up and a new top and I broke the heel off my sandals when I ran off,' Misty looked down at her scratched legs. 'I came looking for you but you weren't here then I fell asleep on your bunk.'

'No harm done. You have a lie down while I put in a quick call to the site doctor. Tell me, Misty,' she said as she punched in the number, 'you won't be in trouble or anything like that, but your father and I found a ransom note . . . '

'It was only a joke,' Misty looked ready to start crying again. 'Kelly and I thought if one of us was going to run away we would need some money, but we'd never have used it. We really were being silly. I thought Kelly had torn it up.'

'Don't worry about it,' Andi smiled down at Misty. 'There's Doctor Suzie now,' she said, catching sight of the middle-aged woman striding across the forecourt towards the camper van. 'Want me to make myself scarce?'

'Stay, please?' Misty grabbed out at Andi's hand as Doctor Suzie tapped on the door.

'Suzie,' Andi murmured a greeting,

'could you give Misty the once over? She's distraught. The boyfriend ditched her in a rather cruel manner.'

'And you want me to make sure everything's all right?' Suzie nodded in her competent manner. 'Leave it to me. Glad you found her. The place has been in an uproar. Jas is baying for someone's blood.'

'I've a nasty feeling that by the end of the day, it might be mine,' Andi said.

'Nonsense. You found her. Remember? You'll be the heroine of the hour.'

'Hope you're right. Misty wants me to stay. I'll make some tea in the galley shall I?'

'Good idea.'

Suzie was back in the galley a few moments later. 'She's fine and you've done a good job calming her down. I've given her a mild sedative. The only thing that's been hurt is her pride. With a bit of tender loving care she'll get over it.'

'Good.' Andi warmed the teapot.

'She's nipped next door by the way.

Something about nail varnish?'

'I hope Holly will forgive me,' Andi made a face. 'Don Budge's girlfriend gave her a new bottle. I sort of promised it to Misty.'

'Don't you think you're in enough trouble without adding to it?' Suzie asked raising her eyebrows as she snapped shut her case. 'Want me to put the word round that Misty's been found safe and well?'

'Please.'

'Will do.'

There was a draught behind her as Suzie opened the camper van door and went out. She heard someone yank open the door again.

'Did you find the nail varnish on your shelf?' Andi called through. 'Tea and biscuits in the galley. I'll be out in a minute.'

'I don't know what's going on here,' Jas began, 'but I've just bumped into Doctor Suzie and she informs me that Misty was hiding in your camper van all along.'

'Yes, that's right.'

'So that ransom note was your doing? What were you going to do? Drive away in the camper van while we were all at rehearsals? Pity your plans went wrong.'

'Hold on a minute,' Andi began.

'I know you're short of money, but don't I pay you enough?'

'What are you talking about?'

'Bella was right in her suspicions, wasn't she? Like a fool I stuck up for you.'

'What do you mean?' Andi's voice was a hoarse rasp. Her mouth was almost too dry to speak.

'I thought you were different.' Jas was raging at her. 'Well, more fool me for trusting you. I won't make the same mistake again. I'm sorry your plans went wrong, Ms Cox. Now I'd like you to pack your bags.'

'What?'

'Don't you understand me? I want you off the premises.'

'What about Misty?'

'I think you've caused her enough

grief, don't you?'

'But you don't understand.'

'I understand very well and if you're not off the premises in five minutes, I'll call security and have them personally escort you down to the gates.'

'That won't be necessary.' Andi tossed back her hair, her anger rising to the same level as Jas's. 'I won't bother to pack my things. You can send them on to me. But before I go,' she began, 'since we're into plain speaking here, there are one or two things I have to say to you.'

'I don't want to hear any more of your excuses.'

'I don't intend to make excuses. I intend to tell you exactly what I think of you.'

Jas looked taken aback, but before he could protest, Andi pressed on, 'I thought you were different too. I thought you were kind and caring and I was growing to,' Andi hesitated, 'like you, but you're nothing more than another superstar who believes his own publicity. Your over-inflated ego has coloured your judgement and turned you into a suspicious and mean minded person. You think everyone is out for what they can get in this world. First you accuse Kelly, now me.'

A small muscle tightened Jas's jawline. By now Andi was so fired up, she didn't care what she said. 'Yes I am short of money. I admit it. There's no shame in that. But I'm prepared to work for my wages. I don't 'do' celebrity children kidnaps to supplement my income. I believe in a fair day's work for a fair day's pay. Something you seem to find difficult to understand.'

She snatched up her handbag.

'So there you have it. I can't say it's been a pleasure knowing you, because frankly, it's been a pain. Good luck with the concert. I know I shouldn't say this but I hope you get the biggest attack of stage fright ever when you walk on stage to sing. I hope your voice gives up on you and you stand there gaping like a goldfish looking like the fool you are.'

Aware her parting shot had been nothing more than a cheap jibe, Andi half turned to apologise already full of contrition. That was the trouble when her tongue ran away with her. She didn't know when to stop.

'Sorry, I didn't mean that,' she began.

'I'd say you meant every word,' Jas said slowly and clearly.

It was impossible to read the expression on his face. Andi gulped. In the confines of the camper van, he was standing too close to her. She began to feel uncomfortably hot.

'Where are you going?' he asked.

'What's it to you?' Andi asked nursing a faint flare of hope that he was going to say he realised he had been wrong about her and ask her to stay.

'I need to know where to send your things.'

'New Zealand,' she retaliated, 'and if you want the money for the courier you can go and sing for it.'

She pushed past him. The van rocked

as she slammed the door behind her with a satisfying bang. Turning to look neither right nor left, Andi strode towards the security gates, hot tears scalding the back of her throat.

Andi's New Family Welcome Her

'Just let me get my hands on him.' Hermione's newly styled hair-do shook with outrage. 'I shall never listen to his music again. The man is deranged. I've a good mind to sue. Want me to find you a brief?'

Andi was beginning to wish she hadn't been so open about what had happened at March Manor, but she'd had to provide a reason as to her sudden appearance at Pipkin Cottage and Hermione soon winkled the whole story out of her.

Andi wasn't sure she had made much sense to Al as she'd tried to tell him what had happened, but he'd insisted she borrow a pool car, promising he would square things with Jas later.

After he'd waved her off, Andi had

driven full pelt to Pipkin Cottage. Before Andi could insert her key, the door had been yanked open by a delighted Hermione, whose happiness at seeing Andi again had soon turned to indignation when Andi appraised her of the reason for her sudden arrival on her father's doorstep.

'What's Jas's number?' Hermione had already picked up the telephone.

'No.' Andi snatched the receiver out of Hermione's hands and put it back in the cradle. 'Least said, soonest mended, don't you think?'

'That's never been my way,' Hermione began. 'I mean he can't go about the place accusing my girl of goodness knows what. He may be a superstar but that doesn't mean he can treat you like dirt.'

'Tell me about your plans.' Andi managed to hustle a still protesting Hermione into the kitchen.

'Blow the coffee,' she switched off the kettle. 'Let's have a glass of wine in the garden.'

'Where's Dad?' Andi looked round as Hermione place a bottle of white wine and some nibbles on a tray.

'Clearing up one or two last minute bits and pieces at the college.'

As a diversion tactic it had been a stroke of genius. Andi listened attentively for the next twenty minutes as Hermione delivered a blow-by-blow account of the reception she had planned. The service itself was going to be a small family affair, but by all accounts the reception was going to be the social event of the village.

'Charley's friends are doing the food. I'm not having any of that fancy finger stuff. We're having a proper sit down meal, eighty of us in all. Darling, you have got to see the cake. It is a creation beyond description.' Hermione almost knocked over the bottle of wine as she made a sweeping gesture with her hands. 'It's in the shape of a French chateau.'

Andi gulped. 'Did you say a chateau?'

'That's right. I adore France, don't

you?' She clasped her hands together in delight. 'Why didn't I think of it before? When I get back from honeymoon, we'll take the shuttle to France for the day. My first husband was half French. His family came from The Loire Valley, near Tours. I lived there for a time.' A fleeting sadness crossed Hermione's normally happy face.

'Hermione?' Andi put out a concerned hand.

'Sorry,' she sniffed. 'Always get a bit emotional when I remember Reggie.' She rubbed at her nose with a tissue. 'He died when Charley was only three. You know,' Hermione's voice was muffled, 'I never thought I'd find love again.' She gave a shamefaced smile, 'but the moment I saw Daniel I fell in love for the second time in my life. I know I sound like a silly teenager, but you see Reggie would have liked him too and there really is no better accolade than that. Darling, you don't mind sharing your father with me do you?'

By now Andi was beginning to wish she had a hankie on board. 'Of course I don't, but it's only a deal,' she turned her reply into a joke, 'if you'll let me share Charley with you.'

When Daniel got home from college an hour or so later, he found Hermione and Andi still out on the terrace, tucking into an enormous pepperoni pizza and laughing together uproariously as Hermione recounted some of her adventures on the streets of Athens when she had been practising her limited knowledge of the Greek language as she tried to track down a particularly ancient Byzantine artefact, the nature of which Andi never did quite discover.

*   ★   ★

The next week passed in a blur of packing, more shopping trips, dress fittings and rehashed seating plans as yet more guests were added to the list. Andi managed to escape to her room one afternoon to send a few e-mails.

Bill Branch had been delighted to hear from her. He was settling down well in his new life and had managed to start up another security agency. There was always a job for Andi any time she cared to join him, he promised her.

Her mother, once she had got over the shock of hearing Daniel's news, had sent down some practical woollen blankets as a wedding gift. Like Andi she had been surprised to learn of Daniel's remarriage. She would not be attending the ceremony she explained due to the long journey involved, but she wished the happy couple well.

Andi printed off the email with relief. She supposed she would have to visit her mother some time in the not-too-distant future, but at the moment there was so much going on in her life she didn't think she would have the time.

Sam too had sent his best wishes. He was currently in America and wouldn't be able to make it home for the wedding, but he had ended his e-mail with a promise to catch up soon.

Andi felt an unexpected surge of warmth as she clicked off. Sam had signed his e-mail with kisses, an unusual gesture from her normally reserved brother. Perhaps the new girlfriend he mentioned had softened him up a bit. She hoped so. Her father's remarriage did seem to be drawing the family back together again.

Andi glanced down at the car keys on her dressing table. She really ought to return the pool car to March Manor, but as she didn't have a car of her own at the moment, and Pipkin Cottage was a long way from the nearest public transport, she was in a bit of a quandary.

She could use her father's bike to get around she supposed, but it wasn't always available and the ride into Canterbury would strain her under exercised limbs and she certainly couldn't use it to pedal all the way back from March Manor if she decided to return the car personally.

She decided to send another e-mail to Al, to see if he could come up with any ideas.

* * *

The day of the wedding dawned bright and pleasantly warm. Hermione looked stunning in an oyster satin suit and an outrageous hat. Charley was best man and looked extremely uncomfortable in his new suit.

'I'm used to wearing checked trousers and chef's whites,' he complained as he struggled with his tie. 'Can you help me with this thing?'

'Stand still,' Andi complained as she battled to undo the knot and start again. 'There,' she stepped back to admire her handiwork. 'Now don't touch it.'

'That colour pink suits you,' Charley said as in his turn he straightened Andi's hat that had somehow come adrift, as she'd tended to his tie. 'Mum certainly knows her stuff.'

Hermione had absolutely insisted on buying Andi's wedding outfit and that had been one argument Andi had been unable to win. Her protests had fallen on deaf ears, until in the end Andi realised she would be seriously hurting Hermione's feelings if she didn't give in gracefully.

'You know,' Andi hesitated, 'Hermione is the last person in this world I would have thought of as an expert in Middle Eastern architecture.'

'Me too,' Charley agreed, not in the least put out by Andi's remarks. 'But isn't she fantastic?'

'Yes, she is.' Andi smiled back at him. 'Now come on, brother-to-be, we've got to get our respective parents properly married.'

* * *

The day passed in a dream. Andi's father had looked suitably nervous as Hermione insisted on arriving for the simple ceremony half-an-hour late.

'Didn't want to look too eager,' she hissed at Andi who'd also been in an agony of apprehension in case something had gone wrong at the last minute. She had managed to escape to the steps outside the register office to see why Hermione was being held up.

It was with a sense of relief she saw Hermione's beribboned saloon car rounding the corner.

'Don't you look lovely?' Hermione said as the car cruised to a halt and she emerged resplendent in her wedding finery.

'You too,' Andi responded. 'Now come on. Poor old Dad is as nervous as a cat on hot bricks. He thought you weren't going to turn up.'

Andi gave a devilish wink. 'Glad my strategy worked. Come on then, darling, let's not prolong his agony. Charley,' she ordered her hovering son, 'got the ring?'

'Yes, Mum.'

'Right. Off you go. Now you, Andi, are honourary bridesmaid.'

'What?' Andi protested.

'You didn't think I spent a fortune on that outfit for you to hide yourself away in the back row did you?' Hermione demanded.

That was exactly what Andi had hoped to do. Instead she found herself frogmarched to the front of the proceedings and clutching Hermione's bouquet as she and Daniel exchanged their vows.

The service of blessing that followed was absolutely perfect and by the time the small family gathering made its way to Charley's everyone was ready to party.

To Andi's intense embarrassment Hermione had aimed her bouquet straight at her and Andi had been forced to catch it, amid loud cheers and enthusiastic applause from the other guests.

'Stay as long as you like at Pipkin Cottage,' her father had said before he and Hermione departed for the airport and their flight to Istanbul. 'We'll be away for about six weeks so the place is yours.'

'Thanks, Dad.'

With 'Just Married' streamers trailing from the car, the happy couple drove off from Charley's, Hermione still trying to issue instructions to Andi through the open window about what she would like to do to Jas Summers before her new husband finally managed to quieten her down.

'Had enough for one day?' Charley murmured in her ear as guests began drifting off after the reception. He tugged at his tie in relief. 'Glad I can get rid of this thing at last.'

'I think I have,' Andi admitted, taking off her hat and running her fingers through her hair. 'Fancy a cup of tea at Pipkin Cottage?'

'I can think of nothing I'd like more. Hold on, I'll get us some wedding cake to have with it. I never did get a slice did you?'

Andi shook her head. The afternoon had passed in a non-stop round of introductions and hand shaking with people whose names she had immediately forgotten.

'We'll walk, shall we?' Charley suggested as he reappeared clutching two paper napkins full of generous helpings of wedding cake. 'Think I need to clear my head and Alfie here needs to stretch his legs.'

Her father had left the dog in Charley's care rather than put him in kennels.

'He pines,' Charley explained as he clipped Alfie's collar. 'As long as he doesn't get in the way of things here, it's nice to have him.'

Together they strolled up the hill. As they breasted the rise, Charley undid Alfie's lead and as usual he raced off into the undergrowth. The late afternoon sun was hazy now and midges danced madly in the dying light promising another fine day tomorrow.

'Anyone driving by wouldn't believe their eyes,' Andi said indicating their outfits. 'Me in a pink hat and dress, you in your wedding outfit.'

'Thank heavens we don't have to do it too often.'

Charley stuffed what remained of his tie into his pocket, then linked fingers with Andi as they walked along. Farm machinery droned in the distance.

'Now we're officially related, I'm allowed to hold your hand,' Charley informed Andi as he caught her look of surprise. 'Mum said I was to look after you, so I intend taking my duties in that direction very seriously.'

'Won't your girlfriend be jealous?' Andi asked.

'Haven't got one at the moment,' he admitted. 'It's difficult to build up a relationship working the hours I do. It would take a very special girl to understand that my work comes first.'

'It's the same with me,' Andi said. 'I can be away for weeks on end sometimes more if it's a long assignment. At least, I used to be until I lost my job.'

'Please don't think I'm prying,'

Charley began slowly, 'but Mum mentioned some unpleasantness?'

'I was dismissed,' Andi said flatly, reluctant to go into details.

Now the wedding was over she would have to get down to some serious job application work. Her c.v. would need to be updated and her skills refreshed.

'Well if you ever need a glowing reference, I'm your man,' Charley said.

'Actually I'm thinking of joining my old boss in New Zealand.'

'You can't do that,' Charley protested.

'Why not?'

'We've only just met.'

'I know that but . . . '

'Was it something I said?'

'Of course not.'

'Good. Seriously, though, Andi, New Zealand's a long way off. Don't do anything rash. I mean you've got a whole new family in this country now. We'd all miss you like mad if you left. You can always use my spare room if you're stuck for somewhere to live, and

I can offer you some temporary work in the kitchen to tide you over, and all the free dinners you can eat until you find another job and you won't get a better offer than that.'

'Bless you, Charley,'

Laughing her thanks, Andi threw herself into his arms and kissed him on the tip of his nose.

'Look out,' he protested trying to rescue their slices of wedding cake.

'You know, Charley,' Andi knew her voice was raised but she didn't care. There was no-one down the country lane to overhear them. 'At this moment there's no-one I love more in this world than you.'

A discreet cough from the hedge behind her had Andi whirling round in dishevelled surprise.

'Who's there?' she called out, glad she had the protection of Charley's bulk beside her.

A figure stepped forward out of the shadows.

'Good heavens.' Charley let go of

Andi's hand with undignified haste, dropping what remained of their pieces of cake onto the ground in the process.

'Hello, Andi.'

'Jas Summers,' Charley butted in before Andi could reply. 'Charley Richards. I've been a fan of yours like forever.'

Andi held her breath. If Jas chose this moment to be rude to Charley, she wouldn't be responsible for her actions. Although she'd barely known Charley a month, she loved him dearly. So what if he was overweight and losing his hair? His heart was in the right place and he wasn't about to desert her because times were bad.

Andi didn't know what Jas was doing here, but whatever history they had between them, none of it was Charley's fault.

A tired smile softened Jas's face. 'Thank you, Charley,' he said and sounded as though he meant it.

'Some of the boys at the restaurant have got tickets for your charity concert. Can't wait. Want me to put up some posters in the restaurant? I run *Charley's*.'

'I've heard of it,' Jas said. 'You've got a growing reputation. I'll have my publicity people courier you some advertising literature. Will you be at the concert?'

'Nothing would keep me away.'

'Look forward to seeing you there then. If you mention my name at the gate, the guards will make sure you get a good view.'

'No kidding? I can see I'm going to enjoy having a new sister who can pull strings for me at a Jas Summers concert. I couldn't believe it when she said she worked for you.' Charley's face fell as he realised his choice of words had been a tad unfortunate. 'Er, look, Andi, mind if we take a rain check on that cup of tea? I really should be getting back. There's a lot of tidying up needs doing at the restaurant and I'm afraid,' he looked down at the sugar icing and bits of marzipan sticking to his shoes. 'The cake's off,' he said.

'No,' Andi tried to detain him. 'You don't have to go.'

Charley's eyes swept briefly over the situation. 'I think I do,' he said softly. Then putting out a finger to stroke Andi's chin said, 'Keep in touch. Come on, Alfie,' he whistled. 'Walkies.'

An Unexpected Visitor
For Andi

They both watched Charley make off back down the hill, Alfie barking at his side, his tail wagging madly.

'You look very glamorous,' Jas turned his attention back to Andi as Charley faded from view. 'Your hat's a bit squashed though.'

Andi looked down at the wrecked creation in her hands. She hoped some steam would restore it to its former glory.

'I've been to a wedding. My father's,' she tried to glare up at Jas but it wasn't easy. Her heart was beating its usual tattoo of welcome. 'And before you start accusing me of heaven knows what, Charley was only escorting me back from the reception.' She looked down at the crumbs of cake littering the ground. 'We were going to have a cup of tea.'

'I want you to come back,' Jas said, his voice gentle and entreating.

Andi tossed back her head. 'Shame we can't always have what we want, isn't it? And if you think for one moment I'd come back after all the things you said about me, well, you've got another think coming.'

Jas's eyelashes worked overtime as he blinked hard, a faint flush of emotion discolouring the base of his neck.

'Look, can we talk inside?' he pleaded. 'It's a bit public out here.'

'Scared an army of fans will discover you standing in the middle of a country lane?' Andi taunted him as she arched an eyebrow. 'You're right,' she agreed. 'It's hardly the place for a superstar. So, I suggest you leave. March Manor's that way.'

Andi pointed towards the main road.

'It's not that.' Jas's jaw was stiff as if he had difficulty speaking. 'I've been waiting ages for you. I didn't know where you were.'

'Seeing as my social diary is no concern of yours and I didn't ask you to come here that is not my problem.'

'My problem is,' Jas began to look even more uncomfortable, 'I was nervous before I left so I downed a pot of coffee.'

'I hope you enjoyed it. Now if you don't mind I've got a lot to do.'

'It's a long drive over from Old Haven. We got lost down the country lanes and the journey took over two hours.'

'It's a long drive back too, Jas. So the sooner you start, the sooner you'll arrive. Where's your car?'

'I haven't got one.'

'You mean you walked?'

'Al drove me over. I told him not to wait.'

'Hmm,' Andi agreed. 'You have got a problem. Would you like me to lend you my father's bike? It's a bit rickety but I'm sure it's up to the journey.' Andi couldn't resist adding, 'There's a pump if you should get a puncture on the way and one of those little kit things to mend it. Do you remember those?'

'I don't want your wretched bike,' Jas all but snarled at her.

Andi was beginning to enjoy herself now. To see Jas grovelling in front of her for what she suspected was the urgent need for a comfort break was the perfect end to a perfect day.

'The offer was made in good faith.'

Fuelled by Hermione's generous supply of wedding champagne, Andi was in no mood to accept any more flak from Jas.

All week she had half hoped he would ring and apologise, but when, after the third day, there had been no telephone call from him, she had given him up as a lost cause and set about moving on with her life.

'If you've come to collect the pool car,' Andi swept a hand towards where the vehicle was parked on the grass verge. 'There it is. Sorry I haven't garaged it. Dad doesn't have one. Safe journey home.'

'I don't have the keys, you do and I was rather hoping we could drive back together.'

'Sorry,' Andi stifled a yawn, 'don't think I'm up to going anywhere right now. Although Charley has deserted me I still want that cup of tea.' She pushed opened the wicker gate then hesitated. 'Why?' she asked.

'Why what?' Jas looked baffled.

'Why do you want me to drive back with you? Surely that would take us back to square one wouldn't it?'

'I don't follow.'

'Well if I came back to March Manor with you, someone would then have to drive me back to Pipkin Cottage, then they'd have to drive . . . '

'Stop rambling and listen to me, will you?' Jas's fingers dug into Andi's shoulders as he forced her round to face him. 'We all want you back — on a permanent basis. We don't want you driving away anywhere ever again. Misty went mad when she found out you'd left.'

'Did she let you have it with both barrels?' Andi couldn't resist asking.

'And some.'

'Attagirl, Misty.' Andi grinned up at Jas. 'Hope she made you feel like the worm you are.'

'I thought Doctor Suzie was supposed to have given her a sedative,' Jas protested.

'She did.'

'Well it didn't work on Misty. She left me in no doubt that I had seriously misunderstood the situation.'

'It's a shame you didn't realise that before you started hurling unfounded accusations at me,' Andi retaliated, 'and will you take your hands off my shoulders. You're hurting me.'

'No, and it's no more than you deserve. It's been hell on earth without you.'

'You haven't exactly hurried over here to find me,' Andi pointed out. 'It's been a week.'

'You told me you were going to New Zealand.'

'You didn't fly out there looking for me did you?'

'No, but I e-mailed Bill. He said he

was holding a job open for you and that you were considering his offer but he wouldn't tell me where you were.'

Now the effects of the champagne were beginning to wear off Andi was beginning to remember how angry he had made her, but seeing Jas standing in front of her also reminded her how much she had missed him.

Over the past few days, Hermione had helped her block out the memory of what had happened at March Manor, but now the wedding was over Andi was beginning to feel flat and the memories were flooding back — the fish and chip suppers in Daisy One, the late night snacks in the main kitchen, being covered in plaster when a ceiling had come down on them and Jas singing *Song Of My Heart* to her when it seemed they were the only two people alive in the world.

She bit her lip. Why did he have to look so heart wrenchingly handsome standing before her in faded jeans and an old shirt?

And why were their wires so seriously crossed? There was no way Andi was going back to March Manor only to be accused yet again of dereliction of duty the next time something happened to one of his daughters.

'When I told Misty I didn't have any idea where you were, she completely took me to task and didn't pull any punches.'

'Poor Jas,' Andi felt her first stirrings of sympathy for him. 'You shouldn't have brought your girls up to be so independent.'

'Tell me about it,' Jas raised his eyebrows. 'After everyone had calmed down a bit we set about trying to find out where you'd gone. Ivy said she knew your father's address, but she wasn't giving it out to anyone, until she knew exactly what was going on. You've got some extremely loyal friends.'

'Good old Ivy. I swore her to secrecy. At least I've got one friend I can trust at March Manor. If Ivy didn't spill the beans, how did you find out where I was?' she asked.

'From the e-mail you sent Al.'

'Do you normally go round reading other people's mail?'

'He showed it to me. You put your address on it when you asked him to come and collect the car.'

'And I thought Al was my friend.'

'Please, Andi?' Jas implored. 'I know I said things I shouldn't have but don't you see, when I discovered Misty had been in Daisy One all along, you were playing straight into Bella's hands?'

'I was? How?'

'She's only looking for the slightest excuse to get rid of you. There was no way I could keep Holly quiet on that one. You know what a chatterbox she is. Bella hasn't found out yet, but it's only a matter of time before she does.'

'Then she's not going to be best pleased to find I've come back, is she?'

'You've got Misty batting on your side.'

Jas gave another wince of discomfort.

'You'd better come inside,' Andi said,

finally taking pity on him. 'The bathroom's upstairs. I'll be in the kitchen.'

She unlocked the door to Pipkin Cottage and throwing off her coat and putting her hat on the dresser, set about busying herself washing up the vast array of crockery and glasses that had built up in the sink during the course of the morning.

It helped to do something routine with her hands while she tried to make sense of all that was going on in her head.

A few moments later a refreshed Jas appeared at her side and taking a tea towel off the hook began drying up. Neither of them spoke until Andi was wiping down the draining board.

'That's something I haven't done in years,' Jas admitted as he hung the towel over the dryer.

'Glad to see it's a knack you haven't forgotten.'

There were dark circles under his eyes and he hadn't shaved. As he smiled at her she found herself wanting to stroke the stubble on his chin. Appalled by the treachery of her thoughts, Andi turned away from him and opened the back door to let in a breath of evening air. It was doing her temperature level no good to be so near Jas Summers, but she was blowed if she was going to fan herself in front of him.

'There's something I haven't told you,' he said coming up behind her. Her face felt hotter than ever.

'What?' Andi spun round and almost found herself in Jas's arms.

'Holly's poorly.'

'What?'

'Ivy's been nursing her. She says it's only a bit of fever but Holly's not getting better.'

'What does Doctor Suzie say it is?'

'At first she thought it was a grumbling appendix but now she thinks she's pining for you.'

'That is below the belt, Jas,' Andi was more than glad she had opened the door. Her temperature was now rocketing off the scale from a combination of the nearness of Jas's body to hers and because she would never forgive herself if anything happened to Holly.

'Misty's taken over looking after the animals for her, but she's not a natural. She's been thrown by Poppet and got a bruise,' Jas said. 'The rabbit's gone on hunger strike and won't touch his lettuce and we think Kitty's in trouble.'

Andi ignored the surge of longing to see everyone again building up inside her. From the picture Jas was painting of life at March Manor it looked like things were getting out of control on all fronts.

'Anything else to tell me?'

'Loads. Ivy's grumbling because there's no-one to help sort out her day. I didn't realise you helped her out quite so much.'

'I do, but only sometimes,' Andi admitted.

Ivy had never been the most organised of people and often needed direction, a fact that wild horses would never have drawn out of Andi.

'Frankly, we're in a mess,' Jas admitted.

'It sounds like it.'

'Are you going to take up Bill's offer of a job in New Zealand?'

Andi hesitated. 'I haven't decided yet.'

'If I promise we'll all be on our best behaviour at March Manor will you come back?'

'I don't want you on your best behaviour.'

'What then?'

'I'll come back if . . . '

'You will?' Jas butted in before she could finish.

'If there are certain ground rules.'

'Anything you say.'

'Misty has to be found something constructive to do. It doesn't look like Kelly's coming back from Germany in the short term and Misty's feeling left out of things. That's why she's moping around the place causing trouble and falling in love with unsuitable boys.'

'Agreed. We're always desperate for stagehands so I'll put her on the team and make sure she works hard. She knows enough about the business to get stuck in. What else?'

Andi took a deep breath. 'In your ex-wife's absence I have full responsibility for the children and my word is law.'

'You've got it now.'

'Only until something goes wrong. Jas, I've been ejected from the premises twice. The first time Bella couldn't get me away from her daughters quickly enough and the second time, well,' she hesitated, 'my feet hardly touched the ground when Misty disappeared did they?'

Jas's long eyelashes swept up and down several times. It was only by exercising the greatest of self-control that she didn't throw herself in his arms and tell him how wonderful it was to see him again. But there was too much at stake here to go down that route.

'What can I say?' Jas said. 'I was so worried about Misty, thinking the worst had happened to her. After you found her all I could think about was how Bella would make mileage out of the situation.'

'Let's cross that bridge when we come to it, Jas.'

'I live in dread that she'll find out about the ransom note.'

'She won't.' Andi eased herself away from Jas and walked out onto the terrace.

She heard him follow her outside.

'How do you know?'

'Because it was Kelly and Misty's doing.'

'They wrote it? But why?'

'I don't think they meant anyone to read it. Misty told me she thought Kelly had destroyed it. To be honest, I think they were bored and being a bit silly. But you needn't worry that Misty will tell any one. I've sworn her to secrecy.'

'Thank heavens Holly doesn't know about it, is all I can say.'

'As we're the only two people apart from Misty who does, I don't think Bella will ever discover the truth.'

'That's a relief.' Some of the anxiety left Jas's face.

'When is she due back in this country — Bella?'

'I'm not sure,' Jas admitted. 'I've heard a rumour that this latest trip to Hong Kong isn't entirely business. She's grown rather close to one of her male partners and her last e-mail said they were taking a short break over the border to Canton. A friend of hers runs sightseeing tours and she said she was going to be out of touch for a while.'

'Will she back in time for the concert?'

'I don't know for sure. Do you want me to find out for you?'

Andi shook her head. Hearing Bella might be otherwise engaged in her personal life was an immense relief.

'Then you'll come back?' Jas asked as the silence lengthened between them.

'As long as I have your promise that you'll stick to all the other conditions.'

'Done. Shall we go back now?' Jas asked eagerly.

'I'm hardly dressed for the part.'

Andi looked down at her styled pink dress. It was stained with the remains of wedding cake and would need a good clean before she wore it again — if ever. On the dresser she could see her hat too was looking decidedly squashed from one too many enthusiastic an embrace.

'You do look a bit of a mess,' Jas agreed.

'The Richards family are a very physical lot,' Andi said with a rueful smile.

'Sounds like it was a good wedding to me.' He picked up a photo off the shelf above the cooker. 'Is this your father?'

'And that's his new wife.' Andi pointed to a waving Hermione, who seemed determined not to be left out of the picture. 'She's also Charley's mother.'

'I can see the resemblance.'

'By the way, I think I should warn you,' Jas looked up, 'Hermione's out for your blood.'

A look of alarm crossed Jas's face. 'Why?'

'All I can say is, you'd better not try accusing me of kidnap again in her presence.'

'Understood.' Jas nodded.

'Hermione's fiercely loyal and you came a stone's throw from being strangled with your own microphone cable.'

'We don't have such things these days.'

'Try telling Hermione that.'

'Right,' Jas looked suitably solemn as he asked, 'Do you want me to make that tea while you change?'

'I could with some sandwiches too,' Andi called from the hallway.

'Didn't they feed you at this wedding?' Jas began looking round for the bread bin. 'In Ireland you're not allowed to leave the table until you can't eat another morsel of food and then some.'

'It was the same at Charley's. Trouble was Hermione had got me down as some sort of guest of honour and every time I raised my fork to my mouth, people kept coming over to me to introduce themselves.'

'Now that I can understand. Our lot are the same.'

'They all wanted to hear about you too. I told them you were a . . . '

'What was that?' Jas demanded as Andi opened the bathroom door and turned on the taps, grinning to herself. 'What did you tell them about me?' he shouted up the stairs.

'I'll be down as soon as I've had a bath,' Andi poured some aromatic oil into the hot water. 'There's some ham in the fridge and you'll find tomatoes in the vegetable rack.'

Andi was looking forward to a good long soak. It cheered her heart to know that Jas cared about what she'd called him behind his back. One day she might tell him she'd said he was a star.

A Return To March Manor

'I do hate to let Jas down, but I'll have to go, Andi,' Ivy's brow was creased with a worried frown. 'I've got no choice. Sandra's only started her new job this week and can't really get time off, and Kelly's that keen. I could hardly get any sense out of her over the telephone last night. Everything has happened so quickly.'

'We'll manage, Ivy,' Andi reassured her. 'Harry will be here to look after your personal stuff and I'll see to the house for you. You've got to go. Kelly needs you. Fancy her winning a scholarship to Frau Schmidt's Academy. You must be so proud of her.'

'It's the chance of a lifetime and she's a very lucky girl to get a place, but she is only sixteen and there's so much paperwork to be sorted out. I don't think Frau Schmidt would have countenanced the idea if Kelly's father hadn't been in Germany as well.

'Dave will have to sign lots of things on her behalf. Then there's the accommodation to be sorted out. Frau Schmidt has recommended a hostel, which she says, is clean and respectable, but I need to check it out. Men are hopeless at that sort of thing and I don't want Kelly staying anywhere unsuitable.'

'Ivy,' Andi attempted to stem the flow, 'you go. Don't worry about a thing. Bob will run you to the airport and I'll look after things here until you get back.'

'I don't know what I'd do without you, Andi, really I don't.'

Ivy was still twittering on as Harry picked up her bag and hurried her down the stairs and outside to where Bob was patiently waiting for her by the car.

He waved a friendly greeting to Andi. It was the first time she had seen him since the day he'd driven her to March

Manor, the day she had met Jas Summers.

'If you don't get a move on,' Harry chided Ivy, 'you'll miss the flight and you've got one of those tickets that you can't exchange.'

His last remark galvanised Ivy into action. Waving madly from the rear window, Andi watched with Harry as Ivy was driven off to the airport by an extremely patient Bob.

Andi had been back at March Manor four days now and with the approaching date of the concert life was more hectic than ever.

Holly had recovered her health with remarkable speed and leapt out of bed the moment Jas and Andi drew up outside Ivy's cottage.

'I've never seen anything like it,' Doctor Suzie remarked the next day, after she'd given Holly the once over. 'She seems as fit as a fiddle. Still, that's children for you, I suppose. Glad to see you back, Andi. Now perhaps we can all get down to a bit of sensible life.'

Holly was off somewhere now busy tending to her animals.

Misty too was a reformed character and had thrown herself into her new job, grandly entitled *stage manager*, with admirable enthusiasm. She was displaying a talent for organisation that even impressed her father.

'You should see her bullying those boys from the college. I mean embarrassing or what?' Jas rolled his eyes. 'They are only volunteers but they're lapping it up, jumping to obey her every command. She's a changed girl. She'll be telling me what to do next.'

'It's the responsibility,' Andi said in reply to Jas's comment. 'Bill gave me the same chance to prove myself and I loved it.'

'We owe you a big one, Andi,' Jas said. 'We're relying on you more and more, now Bella's deserted us.'

There had been an e-mail waiting for Jas on his return from Pipkin Cottage with Andi. Bella had decided to use Hong Kong as her main base for the next six months as she and her partner had won an important new contract. There followed a screed of instructions regarding March Manor, none of which Jas bothered to read.

'Jas,' Andi protested as he tossed the e-mail to one side.

'Never was much of a one for reading,' he explained with his impish smile. 'All that matters is that the girls will be staying here with us. Bella doesn't feel she wants to uproot them again and I agree with her. They're settled here. You're back too, so we are cooking on gas. Now all we have to do is arrange us a charity concert.'

'What about my replacement?' Andi demanded. 'Bella's list?'

'On permanent hold, I'm pleased to say.'

'Are you happy with me taking over some of Ivy's responsibilities while she's in Germany?' Andi asked.

'Of course,' Jas said. 'Why not? You've been running the show from behind scenes anyway as far as I can make out.'

'I won't be able to keep such a keen eye on the girls.'

'Misty's fine these days. I'm not in the least worried about her and Holly's settled down too. She's got her animals and she's sensible enough to come looking for us if there's a problem. We've cleared up all that business with what we thought was a ransom note, so, no worries. You don't mind do you? All the extra work?' Jas asked with a look of concern. 'I mean I know it's asking a lot of you, and keeping house was not what you were employed to do.'

'I can multi task with the best of them,' Andi assured him, 'as long as there's no adverse feedback from Hong Kong.'

'There won't be,' Jas assured her, 'now relax.'

He put out a hand as if to touch her face. Andi flinched, anxious to keep physical contact between them to a minimum and he dropped his hand instantly.

Moments later he was called away by

one of the builders and Andi set about the task of organising the domestic staff. The renovation of the house was progressing well and soon they would need extra workforce to help tidy up the new rooms.

Jas confidently predicted that Andi and the girls would be able to move into their newly decorated bedrooms within the week.

Misty had escorted Andi to their part of the house and proudly shown her the new rooms, 'and,' she opened a door, 'we are all en-suite.'

Andi glanced enviously at the bath. She couldn't wait to try it out. Showers were all very well but after a long hard day on site, she longed for a hot soak.

'I chose the décor myself,' Misty said, indicating the colour washed walls. She had chosen pastel colours, pink for Holly, warm peach for her room and cool mint for Andi's.

The colours should have looked stark, but their plainness made the previously gloomy rooms look much larger. They opened up the vista over the park and Andi had gasped at the panoramic views.

'On a good day you can see three counties,' Misty leaned her elbows on the windowsill next to Andi. 'I hope you like it,' she said anxiously. 'If you don't we can always change it.'

'I love it,' Andi said simply.

Misty glowed with pleasure at the compliment.

'Best get on with my other job then. Bye.'

She slipped off the window ledge and sauntered out of the room.

The concert was now less than ten days away and every morning presented a new challenge. There was a buzz, a sense of excitement in the air. The charity had been given a lot of free publicity on the local radio and the national newspapers had featured wide spreads on Jas's first live concert for several years.

Fans were beginning to camp outside the gates creating a traffic flow problem for the site vehicles and delivery lorries, but Jas wouldn't hear of them being moved on.

'Without them I'd be nowhere,' he insisted as he made sure hot drinks and basic requirements were sent down to them every day. 'With a bit of good will, we can all get along fine together.'

Every so often Andi spotted Don Budge hovering by the stage. Now the differences between them had been settled, Don and Jas were a good team. Andi had heard them practising together and knew they had a winner on their hands with the new song they were creating especially for the concert.

'I want to thank you for looking after Holly the day Misty disappeared,' Andi said to Don.

'No worries.' His greeny blue eyes lit up at the mention of Holly's name. 'She's a pet, isn't she? Jayne was quite taken with her too. Says if Holly ever fancies a holiday in her Ozzie hometown she'll always be welcome.'

In the distance, Andi could hear

Misty issuing strident instructions to members of her volunteer team. With a smile on her face and a hurried, 'Best make myself scarce,' she strolled back to the camper vans.

These days it didn't do to linger too long if Misty was in the vicinity. You were liable to find yourself clutching a pot of paint and a brush in your hand and told to get on with it.

The camper vans needed clearing out before anyone could move into the main house and Andi decided there was no time like the present. It was amazing how much rubbish the girls had collected in the short space of time they had been using Daisy Two.

Andi cupped her hands and called out, 'Holly, where are you?'

'Here.' Moments later she bounded round the corner.

'Come on, we've got work to do.'

'What sort of work?'

'Cleaning sort of work.'

Holly's face fell. 'I was going to exercise Poppet.'

'Not now,' Andi said firmly. 'I want you to tidy up your things.'

'Why?' Holly pouted.

'Because we are about to move into the big house. Tonight you're going to sleep in your lovely new room.'

'Why isn't Misty tidying up her things? She's made a bigger mess than me,' Holly complained.

'Misty's very busy at the moment. She'll do her bit later.'

'It's not fair,' Holly grumbled. 'Why don't you do it?'

'Because I've got enough to do. Now come on.'

Holly dragged her feet. There was no trace of the sweet little girl now as she stomped along beside Andi. In a way Andi was pleased by this fit of pique. A less than perfect Holly somehow made her more human.

'Misty's the favourite these days,' Holly mumbled. 'Daddy's always singing her praises and says he hasn't got time to come and watch me on Poppet.'

'And he hasn't.' Andi opened the

door to Daisy Two. 'It's time you realised, young lady, the world does not centre around Holly Summers.'

'I hate you!' Holly pushed past Andi. 'Don't come in. This is my private camper van and you do not have my permission to enter.'

Andi resisted the urge to scoop Holly up in her arms and give her a big hug. In her little jodhpurs and riding hat she looked so sweet, but it wouldn't do to let the child think she could get away without pulling her weight.

'Very well,' she said, 'but I want your half of the van spotless. I'm relying on you. I'll be over to inspect things later.'

'Yes, yes, yes,' Holly yanked off her riding hat and closed the door firmly in Andi's face.

Kitty was sunning herself on the steps outside and if Andi hadn't known better she could almost have been convinced the cat winked at her.

Back in her own camper van, Andi set about tidying it up. She bit her lip guiltily. Perhaps she had been a bit hard on Holly. Daisy One was no example of good housekeeping either. Who would have thought she could have created such a mess in the space of a few weeks?

She picked up the postcard Hermione had sent her of the Arkeoloji Museum and re-read it with pleasure.

Made it, Hermione had scrawled, her handwriting as flamboyant as her dress sense. *Off to the Grand Bazaar later then a bit of nightlife I think to hone my belly dancing technique. See you're back with Jas. Let me know if you need any help. Lots of love, darling, your wicked stepmother.*

Tucking the card carefully in her briefcase, Andi patted it indulgently. In her own inimitable way, Hermione had drawn her family back together. Both Sam and Andi's mother had insisted they arrange a party in the not too distant future to welcome Hermione properly into the Cox family. Of course it wouldn't be able to hold a candle to the parties Hermione held at Charley's, but Hermione had appreciated the gesture and informed Andi she was already planning a new outfit for the occasion.

Andi picked up Bella's thick file of domestic notes. She would have liked to consign it to her black bin liner with the rest of her rubbish, but decided that wasn't a very honourable course of action and instead added it to the paperwork in her already bulging briefcase.

★ ★ ★

'Holly?' Andi called through the door to Daisy Two an hour later.

'You can't come in,' Holly snapped back at the sound of her voice.

'I'm going over to the main house.'

'I'm not finished,' she said.

'That's all right. You know where I am if you want me. Misty is working down by the stage with Jas. Don't go wandering off without telling anyone will you?'

'I won't.'

Andi could almost hear Holly's raised eyebrows. She hoped it wasn't Holly's turn to enter the difficult phase. So far the child hadn't shown any tendencies in that direction, but after the mercurial change in Misty's behaviour, Andi knew anything could happen.

She lugged her bin liner over to the skip and tossed the rubbish in, then with a last look at Daisy Two, picked up her hard hat, rammed it on her head and went inside the main house.

Holly Causes A Panic

'Not there,' Misty's voice bit through the lazy afternoon as she issued orders to the stagehands regarding one of the speakers. 'Dad'll fall over it.'

'Poor old soul,' one of the backing group quipped, 'at his advanced age do you think we should order him some extra strength glasses and a walking stick to help him find his way around the stage?'

'We could run off some big print instructions too,' someone else guffawed.

'Very funny.' Misty checked her clipboard and ticked off a few items.

'Misty?' A small hand tugged her sleeve.

'Not now, Holly,' she shook her off, 'I'm busy.'

'But it's important.'

'So is this.'

'Andi says we've got to clear out the

253

camper van 'cos we're going to move into our rooms in the house and I'm bored. I don't want to do it all on my own.'

'Yes, that's right, over there.'

Misty strode across the grass. Holly ran after her.

'You're not listening, Misty.'

'Where d'you want these?' A workman asked.

'What are they?' Misty frowned.

'Canvas backed chairs for the VIPs.'

'No idea. Leave them where they are for the minute, I'll sort it later.'

'Right ho.'

She collided with a small tangle of arms and legs.

'Holly, will you please get out of my way.'

'I want to talk to you,' she stamped her foot.

'And I said not now.'

'But . . . '

'Later.' Misty strode off.

'I hate everybody today,' she shouted after her sister. 'You're all horrid.'

'Even me?' said a soft voice behind her.

Holly whirled round, her lip puckering. 'Yes.' She crossed her arms in challenge and glared up into a pair of pale blue eyes.

'Tell you what, I've got nothing to do. Want me to paint your fingernails again? I've got a really cool electric blue colour. We could do our toenails too. That would be fun?'

'Please.' Holly's bad temper disappeared in an instant as she linked hands with Don Budge's girlfriend. 'Have you got any stuff to take off the old varnish? It's gone all chipped.'

'I expect I can find some. My make-up bag is in my car. I had to park outside the gates. There were so many fans in the lane, the security guards wouldn't let me in.'

'I don't mind walking up to the gate. As long as we're back in time to feed the animals.'

'We will be.' Jayne smiled down at Holly. 'No need to worry.'

'Do you think I should tell Daddy or Misty where we're going?' Holly looked over her shoulder. 'I think I'm supposed to. I'm not going to tell Andi because I'm not speaking to her. She was horrid to me earlier.'

'I don't know where Jas is,' Jayne replied, 'and didn't I hear Misty say she was busy? Besides it won't take long to paint our nails. We'll do it in the car then they can dry while we walk back. Come on. Let's hurry.'

In the distance someone began tuning a guitar, as the dress rehearsal got under way. All attention was on the stage as Holly and Jayne ran off into the long grass.

'OK, Misty?' Jas strolled over to where his daughter was busy issuing more instructions into a two-way radio.

'Chill, Dad. Everything's going like a dream.'

'You've done very well,' he congratulated her. 'I can never get this lot to do anything I ask them.'

'The trick is to flutter your eyelashes,'

she giggled, 'that makes them think you like them.'

'So that's where I've been going wrong all these years,' Jas replied with a wry smile.

'Dad?' Misty hesitated.

'What now?' His voice quickened.

'Nothing serious . . . '

'But?'

'You know that e-mail we got from Mum in Hong Kong? When she told us about her new partner?'

'Yes?'

'You don't mind do you?'

'I'm not going to be difficult about it if that's what's worrying you.'

'No,' Misty shook her head. 'That's not what I wanted to talk about.'

'What then?'

Misty took a deep breath. 'It's about you and Andi.'

Jas's eyes darkened in colour and for a moment he didn't speak.

'Dad?' Misty prompted him.

'There is no me and Andi,' he said.

'I know that.' Misty's cheeks looked

rather hot. 'The thing is what I'm trying to say is, I wouldn't mind if there was. I mean, everyone's noticed the chemistry between the two of you.'

'I wasn't aware of any chemistry so how do they know?'

'They talk, mainly around the catering van.'

'And what they don't know they make up. Misty,' Jas looked serious, 'Look, Misty, put the word round. Andi is twelve years younger than me. She is a different generation.'

'Yeah, yeah, you're a dinosaur, but Andi's ex-fiancé was ten years older than her. She was telling me about him when we had that aromatherapy day out last week.'

'Exactly. It didn't work out because of the age gap.'

'It didn't work out because . . . '

'I don't think we should be discussing Andi's private life,' Jas said tersely.

'All I wanted to say is, I don't mind if you should want to become an item and I'm sure Holly feels the same way.'

'I'm very glad I've got your approval.'

The irony was lost on Misty.

'She was telling me how hard it was for her growing up without any qualifications. She didn't pass any exams at school and if it hadn't been for Bill Branch she doesn't know what she would have done.' Misty's voice was full of admiration. 'Isn't she great?'

'I thought you didn't like Andi.'

'I didn't at first and I know I made her life difficult. But we've talked it through and it's fine now.'

'So you're friends now?'

'Yup, we are. Was it Andi's suggestion to give me this job?'

'It was actually,' Jas admitted. 'Don't you like it?'

'I love it. Dad, I want to go into the business. What do you think?'

'That's something else we can talk about another time. Right now we have a concert to organise. I expect you've got a million things to do and I can't sit around while you organise my love life, if I had one.'

259

'You know what, Dad?' Misty said with a quirk of her eyebrow as she leaned forward and patted his cheek, 'I think you're doing a tad too much protesting.'

'And I think you're interfering in things that don't concern you. Now haven't you got any work to do?'

'If you don't like Andi, how come you were such a grump when you thought she'd cut to New Zealand?'

'That is none of your business.' Jas's voice was now tight. 'And I suggest you drop the matter right there.'

'Misty?' a voice called over. 'We need some help.'

'Coming,' she waved to one of the workmen. 'Bye, Dad. See you later.'

Jas watched her saunter through the grass. He realised he had not handled that conversation with his daughter at all well. She'd had the upper hand from the beginning.

Quite without him realising it, in the space of a few short weeks, Misty had turned into a young woman, a poised and confident young woman, who still occasionally forgot her status and lapsed into giggles. A reluctant smile softened his mouth. She was also astute, funny, hard working and beautiful and now she was beginning to lecture him on his love life.

He didn't doubt Andi had played a significant part in the change in Misty. From the start she'd seemed to understand where both his daughters were coming from. Jas had expected more problems, uprooting them from all they had known and dumping them in the middle of the English country-side. Instead they had both adapted remarkably well.

The microphone squeaked into life.

'If there's anybody out there called Jas Summers, would he please present himself on stage? Jas Summers please?'

Jas ambled forward to a show of slow hand clapping. 'All right,' he tried to explain, 'I was taking five and I might add I talking to a beautiful young woman.'

'Might have known it,' the drummer did a quick roll of his drums.

Jas leapt on the stage. 'Right, you lot, time to get this show on the road.'

★ ★ ★

Andi finished unpacking the last of her bits and pieces and looked round the cool room. The bed wasn't made up but everything else was ready for immediate occupation. She glanced across to the en-suite bathroom. What she really would have loved was a steaming bath full of lots of fragrant oil. She and Misty had gone mad at the aromatherapy centre and struggled home with carrier bags crammed with samples of every essential oil the centre provided.

She glanced at her watch. There really wasn't time and it seemed a bit sneaky to indulge in such luxury while everyone else was working their fingers to the bone. There was Holly to check on too. From the way the little girl had been playing up recently, Andi wouldn't be surprised to find she'd abandoned her work in Daisy Two and wandered off to ride Poppet.

'Little scamp,' Andi said with a smile as her suspicions were confirmed. There was no sign of Holly on board the camper van.

Not wanting to make the same mistake as last time, Andi checked Daisy One in case Holly, like Misty, had fallen asleep on her bunk. She saw to her annoyance Holly had dumped two bin liners full of bits and pieces on the floor.

Kitty she noticed had also abandoned the camper van steps. The whole of this side of the house seemed deserted.

Everyone had wanted to hear Jas rehearse so Andi had let most of the household staff have the afternoon off on the understanding they wouldn't leave the site in case of emergency. All of them carried personal bleepers so remaining in contact wasn't a problem.

Andi sighed. It was all very well helping Ivy out on a casual basis, but full term responsibility for the smooth running of the household was quite a challenge. Looking after Misty was no problem these days. The two of them had bonded after Misty thought her heart had been broken. The teenage heart was a resilient organ and to everyone's relief Misty's proved only to be bruised, not broken. These days she was a totally different girl.

The same could be said about Holly too, but unfortunately in the other direction. It was as if the two girls had changed positions. Lately Holly had been growing into a difficult child. Andi trudged up to the paddock fearing another scene with the child as she attempted to drag her back to the van to finish the job.

Poppet was grazing happily and whinnied at her. There was no sign of Holly.

She wasn't with the rabbit either. Andi looked round in exasperation wishing she'd thought to issue Holly with a bleeper. There was nothing else for it, she was going to have to walk all the way down to the rehearsal stage, something she was keen to avoid.

Lately she had taken to staying out of Jas's way. Ever since her return from Pipkin Cottage after her father's wedding, she'd noticed a change in their relationship and tried to put a distance between them.

It was as if Jas had picked up on the change too. They no longer shared intimate fish suppers or nightcaps in the kitchen when the girls had gone to bed. The demands on his time were such that he was often working until late and supper was now a snatched affair eaten on the run.

Was that what was upsetting Holly? Her father had always taken time out to listen to her, but lately everyone had been too busy to indulge the little girl. As she walked down to the lake, Andi realised that she too had been guilty of ignoring her. As soon as Ivy got back from Germany, Andi vowed she would treat the child to a day out.

'Have you seen Holly?' she asked a group of gossiping cleaners.

They all shook their heads. Andi forced herself to remain calm. Nothing could have happened to the child. They'd cleared up all that business with the ransom note. The guards had increased security on the base after fans began camping outside the perimeter fence.

Holly and Misty were in no danger of a stalker latching on to either of them. They were kept well out of the publicity machine. Jas and Bella had always been insistent that their daughters should not feature in any of the photo shoots, so apart from those closest to the family, not many people knew what Jas's daughters looked like.

Andi began to grow impatient. When she found Holly she'd give her a stern talking to. It was time she learned responsibility and that she was not to go off without telling anyone where she was.

'Hi, Andi, what's up?' Misty wandered towards her. 'You're looking hot.'

'I can't find Holly. Have you seen her?'

'Not for some time. She was around earlier, but I gave her the brush off. I was a bit busy and she was getting under my feet.'

'Where can she be? I've tried all the usual places. I was just about to do a circuit of the lake. She might be up there, although she knows she's not supposed to be there without an escort.'

'She mentioned something about cleaning out the camper vans?'

'That's the last time I saw her, well over two hours ago.'

'Jas is on stage, there's nothing I can do at the moment. What say we split up and each search half of the lake?' Misty looked at her watch. 'Meet you back here in thirty minutes?'

'Thanks, Misty.' Andi squeezed her elbow. 'I don't know what I'd do without you.'

'We'll find her, don't worry. Now off you go.'

The Truth Comes Out
At Last

'Any sign of her?' Andi panted up to Misty. She'd been looking for a while now and there'd been no sign.

Misty shook her head. 'This is looking serious, Andi. I don't want to create panic, but we are going to have to start asking around.'

'We could try Al on the gate? She's been known to wander up there if she's feeling lonely.'

'Right, let's give it a go. I'll tell one of the boys we're taking five. I don't want Dad getting worried when he can't find you, me or Holly.'

While she waited for Misty to deliver her message, Andi tried to go through all she'd got. For all her recent recalcitrance, Holly was a homely child. She liked order in her life and wouldn't willingly have deserted any of her pets.

If Holly had gone off, the chances were she wasn't on her own. Who did she trust? Andi realised to her dismay, she didn't know. Until now Holly had been no bother so Andi had rather let her get on with her own little life.

Misty was back by her side. 'I made a few casual enquiries. As you can imagine there was a fair bit of coming and going. No-one's seen anything.'

A nasty suspicion was beginning to niggle away at the back of Andi's mind. Jas had kept to his word and given her a free hand with regard to his daughters but how would he take the disappearance of a second daughter in almost as many weeks? Holly disappearing was a whole different ball game from Misty's adventure. Holly was only seven years old.

'Perhaps we should tell Jas?' Andi suggested, not relishing the prospect of another explosive encounter.

As the date of the concert grew nearer Jas had grown increasingly tense.

It wouldn't take much to send him over the edge. News that Holly had disappeared would do the trick nicely.

'I don't think we should spook Dad while he's in rehearsal,' Misty said. 'He can get pretty uptight. We'll probably find Holly drinking orange juice with the guards.'

★　★　★

'No, haven't seen her,' Al said in reply to Misty's question. 'Only person who's gone through was that Australian girl. She had to park her car back up the lane this morning seeing as there was a bit of a bottleneck.'

'Don Budge's girlfriend?' Andi asked.

'That's the one. I didn't see anybody with her although I was taking a telephone call at the same time.'

'Don Budge?' Misty almost shrieked.

Two pairs of eyes turned on her in surprise. 'Sorry,' Misty gave an embarrassed smile. 'Didn't mean to shout. Er — any of the pool cars up here, Al?

Andi and I need to slip out for a few minutes.'

'Take that one over there,' he indicated one of the run-arounds. 'Going far are you? Only I need to enter it into my ledger. After that incident the other week, your father was most insistent on that one. He wants to know exactly where everyone is at any given time.'

'We're just going into the village. We shouldn't be long.'

Misty bundled Andi into the driving seat. 'Get going,' she hissed.

'Where?' Andi demanded as she turned the key in the ignition. 'What's going on? And what was all that about Don Budge?'

The wrought iron gates slowly opened as Al activated the security switch. A surge of fans waved at them as they drove through.

'I know where he lives. He overslept the other morning and when he didn't answer his telephone I got one of the boys to turf him out of bed. He's way beyond lazy.'

'He and Jas go way back don't they?' Andi screwed up her face as she tried to remember exactly what she knew about Don Budge.

Misty put a hand to her face. 'His girlfriend, Jayne — she's Australian isn't she? You don't think she's going to pretend to be Holly's mother do you?'

'Misty, what on earth are you talking about?' Andi took her eyes off the road, 'and where are we going?'

'Turn left here,' she indicated a slip road, 'and follow your nose.'

Andi did as she was told, trying to control the erratic beating of her heart. 'Do you think Don Budge has abducted Holly is that it?'

'I'm convinced of it.'

'But why? What reason could he possibly have for taking Holly away?'

Misty turned her large brown eyes on Andi. 'He's her father.'

'What?' Andi swerved with shock.

'Careful,' Misty righted the steering wheel. 'You'll have us in the ditch.'

'Run that past me again,' Andi insisted.

'In a minute.' Misty made a gesture with her hands. 'See that farm house over there?' She pointed to a rundown building in the distance. 'That's it. If you weren't looking for it, you'd never know it was there. It's the perfect place to hide out. No-one ever goes there.' She peered through the windscreen. 'And that's Don's car parked outside.' Her voice rose with excitement.

'Don Budge is Holly's father?' Andi repeated Misty's words very slowly.

'Yes.'

'I thought her father didn't play any part in her life.'

'He doesn't. After Brigid, Holly's mother died, he took off to the other side of the world. My grandparents looked after Holly then Dad adopted her. That's about all I know.'

'And that's why Jas and Don Budge don't get on?'

'S'pose so. Don swanned back into Dad's life when the charity concert was first being arranged. I think that's why Dad wanted special security for Holly.

He was scared something like this might happen.'

'Why didn't he tell me?' Andi demanded as a slow anger began to burn inside her.

'I think he thought the fewer people who knew about the relationship the better.'

'I can understand that, but I was supposed to be responsible for her safety for heaven's sake. Surely I had a right to know about this.'

'That's something you'll have to take up with Dad, Andi.' Misty steadied Andi's arm with her young warm hand. 'Whatever happens, I'm here for you,' she said softly. 'I won't let Dad do anything to you.'

'Thanks, that means a lot to me.' Andi's smile was a bit shaky. Misty's news had rocked her foundations. 'But how do you know all this? I mean have you got your facts right? You could only have been a child at the time?'

'My grandfather told me. He never could keep a secret and when there was a party on and the drink was flowing, which was most of the time, he could be a bit indiscreet.'

'Does Holly know who her real father is?'

Misty shook her head. 'I think Grandpa realised he'd said too much after he told me and he swore me to secrecy. You're the first person I've told. I mean Holly knows she's adopted. She knows Jas is really her uncle, not her father, and that his sister was her mother, but that's as far as it goes. Mum knows too, of course, but she's not here and I don't think she's ever told anyone.'

The lane deteriorated into a rutted cart track as they neared the farmhouse.

'How are we going to play this?' Misty asked, for the first time looking a little nervous. 'I don't think Don's dangerous, but I don't know how badly he wants to take Holly home with him.'

'Home?'

'He's been talking about setting up in Australia.'

'You'd better leave things to me when we get inside,' Andi said, her stomach churning nauseously. Jas would never forgive her for this professional lapse and she could understand why.

She had insisted on total control over his girls and he'd agreed, placing his full faith in her, and she had let him down.

Andi was beginning to realise how foolish her impulsive actions had been. Instead of waiting for back up, she'd driven off from March Manor with Misty, not bothering to tell anyone exactly where they were going. She should have told Jas of her suspicions. So what if he had gone ballistic and taken it out on her? His anger was a small price to pay where Holly's safety was concerned. Now through her own stupidity, the child could be in serious danger.

'Of course Don won't hurt Holly. He's her father, and didn't you say Jayne's with them? She loves Holly.' Andi smiled reassuringly at the girl.

'What I suggest we do is, you wait outside for me in the car.'

'No way,' Misty was emphatic on that one. 'I'm coming in with you.'

'That is not a good idea,' Andi objected.

'Yes it is. At the moment, in Holly's eyes you are public enemy number one. That's probably why she went off with Jayne, because you had words with her. I'll always be her big sister. Holly trusts me.'

Hurtful though Misty's words were, they held a ring of truth. Twice now, Andi had let Holly down by disappearing out of her life, once when Bella had arrived out of the blue and then when Jas had dismissed her. Both times the little girl's health had suffered as a result.

'All right,' Andi agreed, determined not to let Holly down a third time, 'but I'm in charge. I make the rules. You don't agree and no deal?'

Misty nodded. 'Deal. You know,' she said, 'I thought life in England was going to be dull. It's not is it? It's exciting.'

'A bit too exciting. Now are you ready? Don't make any noise.'

Misty opened her passenger door very carefully and quietly. Andi did the same her side. Together they tiptoed up to the house.

'I can hear voices,' Misty whispered.

'It sounds like Holly,' Andi whispered back in relief.

'What do we do? Take them by surprise?'

'I suggest we walk in casually. I don't want to alarm Holly.'

The scene that greeted them could not have been more laid back. Holly was sitting at the tea table tucking into a chocolate éclair. Her foot was in Jayne's lap and Jayne was painting her toenails a virulent electric blue.

Don was seated on the far side of the table browsing through a music magazine.

'Misty,' Holly waved her cake in the air. 'I'm having a mega time.' Her face was smeared with cream. 'Would you like Jayne to paint your nails too?'

There was a look of alarm on the Australian girl's face.

'I wasn't doing any harm,' she insisted, dripping blue nail varnish onto the floor.

'I'm sure you weren't,' Andi replied in a soothing voice. 'Only we do need Holly back at March Manor.'

'Don?' Jayne looked across the table.

'She's right,' Don said slowly. 'We only wanted to have a little tea party with my . . . '

Andi made a quick gesture with her hands to stop him speaking.

'With Holly,' he recovered himself quickly. 'You see Jayne and I won't be able to stay for the concert after all. Her father's not well, so we've got to go back to Australia, first thing tomorrow. I wanted to say goodbye, that's all.'

Andi bit down her rising anger. It wouldn't do any good losing her temper in front of the girls, and she didn't doubt Jayne had only been acting on

Don's instructions. She had no idea whether or not Don had intended taking Holly with him, but it looked now as though he was prepared to admit that had not been his intention. It would do no good making accusations that she couldn't prove.

'Finish your cake, Holly,' Andi said firmly.

'My nails aren't dry,' she scowled at Andi.

'They can dry in the car.'

'There you are, my pet.' Jayne capped her nail varnish. 'I'm about finished here. Don't they look lovely?'

'Can I keep that bottle too?' Holly asked. 'To remind me of you?'

'Of course you can.' Jayne passed it over. 'Now you've got to promise me you'll be a good girl and look after all those animals of yours.'

'I will,' Holly assured her, jumping down from the table.

'Don't forget your shoes.' Don stood up.

He handed them to her then gently

stroked her face. 'Goodbye, my pet.'

'Goodbye and thank you for the tea,' she said in a polite little voice.

'My pleasure.'

Over her head Andi's eyes clashed with Don's.

'Thank you,' he mouthed, adding, 'sorry.'

'Come on, everybody.' Andi ushered her little party out of the room. 'We want to get back to March Manor before they send out a search party for us, don't we?'

'Andi?' Holly slipped a sticky creamy hand into hers. 'I'm sorry I was nasty to you this morning, only no-one would come and play with me.'

'That's all right.'

'Jayne said she would paint my nails, only we had to go back to the car to do it. Then she realised she'd left the varnish remover in her house, so we drove over. I had to sneak past Al because I'm not supposed to leave the house. It was ever so easy. I ducked under the window of the hut and he

281

didn't see me when he went to answer the telephone. Isn't Don nice? He said I reminded him of my mother — my real mother.'

Don and Jayne stood in the doorway of the old farmhouse and waved them off. Holly with her nose pressed up against the rear window of the car waved back at them. She gave a little giggle as they disappeared from view.

'I wouldn't have liked going to Australia,' she said calmly.

'Did Don invite you?' Misty asked.

'He asked me if I'd like to go with him and Jayne, but I wouldn't want to leave you and Daddy and Andi of course.' She stifled a yawn. 'I'm tired.'

Moments later she was asleep in the back of the car.

'I don't think we should tell Dad that last bit,' Misty said in a quiet voice. 'Do you?'

'I don't know what to think. At least Holly's safe and Don's leaving the country tomorrow, so he won't try anything else.'

'We haven't been gone that long,' Misty glanced at her watch. 'Hopefully no-one will have noticed our absence.'

As they made their way carefully back to March Manor, any hopes Andi had in that direction were swiftly dashed. As they approached the wrought iron gates to the house she could see Al talking urgently into his two-way radio.

'Look,' Holly woke up on the back seat and scrambled forward to get a better view. 'Can you see the flashing blue lights, Andi? It's the police.'

'There's Nothing More To Say'

'Didn't you realise I was worried sick?' Jas paced the floor. 'I didn't know what had happened to you' he put his arms around her and hugged her close. She could feel his erratic heartbeat against hers. 'Don't disappear on me again.'

She pushed him away, feeling faintly embarrassed. It only needed Misty to wonder what all the noise was about, open the door and discover Jas and Andi locked in each other's arms.

'You were worried sick?' Andi retaliated in disbelief, still trying to recover from the strength of Jas's embrace.

'Of course I was. I was afraid something like this might happen, ever since we found that wretched note in Daisy Two.'

'I thought we'd agreed that was a hoax.'

'I know, but when I went looking for you and found Holly's bits and pieces stuffed in sacks in your camper van and no sign of my daughter, what was I supposed to think had happened?'

'I don't know. Why don't you tell me?' Andi asked quietly. 'I'd really like to know.'

'I thought you were going to drive away with her or something.' Jas ran a hand through his hair. Yet again he looked as though he hadn't shaved.

'We've already done that one, Jas, with Misty, or had you forgotten?'

'I know. I'm sorry. I over-reacted. I always get hyper and have panic attacks before a performance — even now after all these years of live gigs. It's something I've never grown out of.'

'Having failed with Misty you thought I was going to have another go by abducting Holly. Is that what you are trying to say?'

'No, of course not.'

'What then?'

'I couldn't get my head around the

situation. I know I wasn't making sense. I don't think the police could make out what I was talking about.'

'And you're not making much sense to me either.'

Jas's face was hollow with anguish but Andi felt no pity for his plight. All her warmth towards him vanished in an instant. Yet again it appeared he was accusing her of threatening to kidnap one of his daughters.

'And you're right about not thinking straight. If I had wanted to abduct Holly, then can you tell me why I didn't drive off with her in the camper van while you were all rehearsing down by the lake? No-one would have discovered our disappearance for ages. And while you're at it, can you also please explain why I would want to take Holly away from you?'

'I don't know and will you keep your voice down. The girls might hear you. They're only across the way.'

'Jas, I don't care if they do. I've had it up to here with your accusations.'

They were both breathing heavily as they faced each other across the room.

Andi had suffered an hour's intensive interrogation by the police and if it hadn't been for Misty's support and back up she wasn't at all sure they might not have locked her up for the night.

Keen to play down the significance of Don Budge's role in the drama, Andi's story about Don's girlfriend, Jayne, and the painted toenails had sounded weak even to her own ears, but eventually the police had taken the view that no harm had been done, and as Jas wasn't pressing charges against her, had finally left the premises.

The paparazzi had had a field day by the iron gates, snapping pictures of everyone who passed through. Andi dreaded to think what the next day's headlines would be.

March Manor had been buzzing with rumours and counter rumours all evening and as the dress rehearsal was abandoned for the day, excited groups of workers were busy discussing exactly what they thought had gone on. Everyone had a theory and each one was more outrageous than the one before.

Jas it seemed had called for a break soon after Andi and Misty had left. Not finding either of the girls to dispense much needed drinks and refreshments to the staff he had gone in search of them.

That was when he realised Holly was missing as well. He'd organised a full-scale search of the grounds, then when that had thrown up nothing and Al had told him he'd last seen Andi and Misty driving off towards the local village, Jas decided to alert the police.

'And when were you going to tell me about Don Budge?' Andi demanded.

An uneasy look narrowed Jas's eyes. 'What about Don Budge? I don't know what you mean.'

'Yes you do, but I haven't got it in me to listen to any more of your lies, so to save time I'll enlighten you. Don Budge is Holly's father.' Andi spoke slowly and clearly. 'When he reappeared on the scene you were concerned that he may try and claim rights to Holly, so that was why you wanted a security guard to look after your girls. You probably thought that silly ransom note Kelly and Misty concocted was a veiled threat from him, didn't you?'

'It passed through my mind, yes.'

'You knew all along it was nothing to do with me.'

Jas turned away from her as if unable to look Andi in the face.

'How did you find out about Don?' he asked.

'Misty told me. I'm glad at least one member of the family trusts me enough to tell me the truth.'

'I couldn't tell you.'

'Why not?'

'Because Bella didn't want Holly to know.'

'It's no secret. Holly knows she is adopted.'

'Bella didn't want Holly to know that Don Budge is her father, not yet anyway.'

'Why not? He's not a criminal is he? And she's got to find out one day.'

'Before we were married, Don was an old boyfriend of Bella's.'

'So?'

'Her parents didn't approve of the relationship and so they split up. Bella started going out with me on the rebound, but I really don't think Bella ever got over Don Budge. That's why she likes to pretend Holly is her child, hers and Don's, and not my sister's.'

'It sounds a bit far-fetched to me,' Andi said, 'but even if it's true, you could have trusted me with your secret.'

'I wanted to, but I'd promised Bella I wouldn't tell anyone.'

'As it was, your actions almost endangered the safety of your child.'

'I realise that,' Jas said in a quiet voice. 'I was scared something like this might happen. That's why I called in the police. I'm sorry.'

'Sorry isn't enough. None of your family history concerned me, but I got the blame.'

'I realise I got things seriously wrong, Andi, when it comes to you, I don't seem to think straight.'

'Now what do you mean?'

'That first day we met, I couldn't believe you'd come to look after my children. I was expecting, I don't know, someone a bit more dragon-like I suppose. I half fell in love with you then. You looked so vulnerable. You looked a real woman, not at all like the spoilt wives of business friends I'd been used to mixing with. They were all make-up and hair-dos. You were different — natural, lovely, uncomplicated.'

Andi could feel the tension in the room tighten.

'You promised,' her voice caught in her throat, she shook her head in an effort to clear the blockage, 'to trust me. Why can't you trust me?'

'I do.'

'That's just it, Jas, you don't.'

Jas made a half movement towards Andi then stalled.

'Do you think we can talk about this

after the concert?' he asked, 'please?'

'You mean it's not important enough to talk about now?' Andi's anger flared up again.

'No, that isn't what I mean at all,' Jas protested.

'In case it has escaped your notice, the police were a hair's breadth away from arresting me tonight.'

'I wouldn't have let them do that.'

'When were you going to stop them? You raced off with Holly, leaving me to their mercy in that makeshift incident room.'

'I wanted to make sure she wasn't traumatised by the incident.'

'And I wanted to keep Don Budge's name out of the affair, and Jayne's, that's why my story was so flimsy. I was thinking on my feet. I was being loyal to you, Jas, and the girls, and Bella too. I covered up for all of you and what thanks do I get?'

'Please, Andi, I can't talk about this now.' Jas put his hands to his forehead.

Andi tossed back her head. 'In that

case, there's nothing more to say is there?'

'I do trust you, Andi. The girls are happy with you and even Bella's dropped her resistance to having you look after everyone.'

'And I'm supposed to be grateful for that?'

'What else can I say?'

'There's a whole lot more, but as you don't think the time is right, then I suggest you go.'

'Andi . . . '

'Now.'

'What are you going to do?' Jas asked.

'Ivy's due back tomorrow from Germany. She can take care of the girls until you get someone else.'

'You're not leaving?' Jas looked aghast.

'What else do you expect me to do? There's no future for me here, if every time one or other of the girls does their own thing I get the blame. Don't worry, by the way. I will honour my confidentiality clause. You can trust me not to sell my story to the tabloids.'

The girls were settled in their rooms and although it would break her heart to do it, she had to slip away quietly before anyone tried to stop her. Holly might have another of her little funny turns, but she would get over it. Someone else would come and take Andi's place, someone efficient, who didn't go around in old skirts and lose control of her charges. Soon everyone would forget all about Andi Cox.

'You can't do this, Andi.'

She jumped at the sound of Jas's voice behind her.

'I thought you'd gone.' She shook his hand off her shoulder.

'I'm no good at the personal stuff before a concert. I get so wound up. Everyone knows to stay out of my way. Please, please don't leave.'

'I have to, Jas.' She couldn't trust herself to look at him. If she did, he might see in her eyes the love she felt for him and the Andi Coxes of this world did not go falling in love with superstars.

'Then there's nothing more to say,' he replied slowly, 'if you really mean to leave.'

'I do.'

Andi snapped shut her case.

'Where will you go?'

'Don't worry. You won't have to come and fetch your car back. I'll order a taxi.'

'You haven't answered my question,' Jas said.

'This time I really am off to New Zealand. At least Bill appreciates me. Goodbye, Jas. Hope the concert is a success. Knock 'em dead.'

At this point her voice almost gave out on her. Not trusting herself to look back, Andi heaved her suitcase off the bed and careful not to make too much noise manhandled it out of the room.

The Final Song

The crowd surged forward with a cheer as the gates swung open. Andi had spent the last three hours camped out on a verge drinking endless mugs of tea and eating biscuits to keep up her strength.

The temptation to gatecrash Jas's concert had been too great to resist. Charley had been unable to attend the concert due to a last minute booking at the restaurant and had offered Andi his ticket.

Pulling her woollen hat down to disguise her hair and hunching inside her waterproof jacket she battled through the gates with everyone else, averting her eyes from the security guards scanning the crowds.

The press were out in force and flash cameras were going off in all directions. Andi didn't know how Jas had done it, but no mention had been made of what had happened to Holly in the papers. A political scandal had broken out the following day and to her relief all other news had been swept off the front pages.

Holding her breath as her ticket was scanned, Andi kept her eyes fixed firmly on the ground. Moments later she was passed through. Her chest hurt as she stopped holding her breath and gave a sigh of relief.

A group of students in front of her linked arms and began chanting *Song Of My Heart* as they trudged down to the lake.

It was hot inside her jacket, but Andi didn't dare remove it in case someone recognised her.

'Sorry I can't close up the restaurant and come with you,' Charley had apologised, as they were finishing off in the kitchen the night before. 'I'm a big lad. Can't fight to save my life but my bulk might scare anyone off if they should decide to turn nasty.'

'Thanks, Charley, but I think I'll be all right and tomorrow's booking is important to you. I should really stay and help you.'

'Wouldn't hear of it,' he brushed aside her offer, 'I've got more than enough students willing to earn some extra money.'

'Who is it for again?'

'Um, the charity people, the ones running Jas's concert.'

'I thought he was holding the after-concert party up at the manor.'

'Don't know what Mum's going to make of all this business with Jas when she gets home,' he said, changing the subject as he poured out their cocoa.

Chatting about the day, when everyone else had gone home was a nightly ritual. When Andi had crash landed on Charley a week earlier, he hadn't asked any questions. He'd installed Alfie as guard dog at Pipkin Cottage, then left her alone for a few days, until she'd crept into the kitchen one evening to offer her services.

'You haven't mentioned it to her, have you?' Andi asked.

'Wouldn't dare. She would probably cut short her honeymoon to come to your rescue. You know, she thinks the world of you. I should be jealous of you, but I'm not because I do too, and personally I think Jas Summers needs his brains tested.'

'Charley,' Andi chided him. 'Five minutes in your company and I feel on top of the world again.'

'Want to talk about it?' he asked.

'Do you mind if I don't?' To talk about Jas behind his back still seemed disloyal.

'Understood,' Charley nodded, 'but if you ever want a shoulder to cry on then I'm your man.'

Andi had welcomed the hard work of serving in the restaurant, the late nights, even doing the washing up. She was so tired by the end of the evening, she always crashed into bed and fell asleep the instant her head touched the pillow.

Charley had tried plying her with food but her appetite had deserted her.

'You've got to keep up your strength,' he insisted as his efforts to tempt her to a slice of cake looked like meeting with failure.

'I know, Charley.'

Just to please him she managed a few mouthfuls of the coffee and nut gateau. Delicious though it was, Andi couldn't finish the slice. Charley shook his head in dismay.

'You've got to do better than that when Mum comes home.'

Thinking of Charley and Hermione helped keep Andi's mind off Jas. Being back at March Manor brought the memories rushing out of cold storage. She smiled as she remembered their shared fish and chip suppers and the impromptu concerts down by the lake.

She missed Misty more than she could have imagined and little Holly too, even thinking about the animals brought a lump to her throat.

The early evening smells of the wild

flowers in the hedgerows and the background noises of the last minute practice session before the concert, heightened the atmosphere as the crowd trudged along. The gasp of surprise and more cheering up front alerted Andi to the fact that the leaders had come to the clearing and spotted the house.

With whoops of joy they began running back down the other side of the hill anxious to stake their claim to the best view.

Breaking away from her group, Andi was careful not to be seen as she positioned herself under the trees. The leaves made a good hide and from where she was standing, she could glimpse Holly and Misty sitting in the part of the garden, roped off for VIPs. Their names had been crudely painted onto the back of the canvas seats. Her heart contracted at the sight of them again.

Holly looked so sweet in her sparkly top and jeans and Misty was wearing the dress Andi had bought for her on their day's shopping spree.

It was almost too much for Andi. She gnawed at her knuckles to stop herself from calling out to them. Harry and Ivy were there too and Andi knew she was going to have to move unless she wanted to give the game away by waving at everybody.

She shuffled through the trees, further back into the shade. It was a warm evening and under cover of the foliage, she felt safe enough to remove her woolly hat and undo the buttons of her coat.

The gardens were now full to capacity and as everyone began to settle down the warm up group swung into their routine. Everyone began dancing and singing along to the music and Andi longed to join in but every so often she was forced to duck down as guards and sniffer dogs routinely patrolled the grounds. Andi was glad it wasn't raining. Crouching in the under-growth, she would have got absolutely soaked if it had been.

Someone had decorated the gardens with fairy lights and tables were already being laid out for the party afterwards. Andi frowned. All the charity people were here and they didn't look as though they were moving on later. Some were tucking into sandwiches and others were passing round plates of nibbles and drinks.

Andi began to suspect Charley had given up his ticket for her. The concert had been a sell-out for weeks. There was no way Andi would have got her hands on a last minute return. They were like gold dust.

Now Andi came to think about it, Charley had over insisted she come to the concert tonight. He must have suspected her disappointment at not being able to attend and sacrificed his ticket for her. Why hadn't she realised earlier?

Andi looked round the bushes. It was too late to do anything about it now, but she firmly intended to challenge

Charley in the morning.

The wait for Jas to come on stage seemed interminable and Andi wondered if he was having his usual attack of backstage nerves. The backing group played another number then a female singer did a solo. The crowd began to grow restless and Andi could feel the tension mount.

She didn't see Jas come on the stage but from the volume of the roar that arose from the crowd she knew he had arrived. She peered through the trees, and there he was. He was wearing dark cut jeans and an Irish green top, the colours he always wore on stage because he said they gave him luck.

'Hello Old Haven,' he greeted them.

The crowd roared back at him.

Jas displayed no trace of nerves as he swung into his opening routine. Then the band played number after number of all the crowd's favourites. Looking at Jas as he performed, Andi could not believe that this was the man who had helped her unblock the shower unit on her camper van, gone looking for the rabbit with her when he'd escaped from his hutch and cooked the two of them a bacon and egg breakfast the night after they'd spent hours trying to clear up the mess when a wall had collapsed unexpectedly, bringing down half the ceiling with it.

Forgetting where she was and only wanting to join in the magic of the moment, Andi began clapping her hands and dancing with the music, there was plenty of time tomorrow to remember that Jas had broken her heart and that her time with him was past. Tonight was for enjoying.

Eventually, sensing something was about to happen, the crowd fell silent.

'Thank you, ladies and gentleman,' Jas picked up the microphone. 'What a lovely reception for an old timer.'

His comment was met with enthusiastic cheering.

'I'd like to thank all my team for their unstinting hard work, which they did most of the time without complaint.' Jas grinned at his backing group, then down at his daughters. 'My family, of course, and all the volunteers who were more than put through their paces by my very formidable daughter. Can't think where she gets it from.'

Groans from the stage were mixed with the cheers that greeted that remark as Misty stood up and waved her acknowledgement.

'And now the moment you've all been waiting for.' Jas paused. 'This concert is in memory of my beautiful sister, Brigid.'

The crowd fell silent.

'But first of all, I've an announcement to make. I'm not very good with words so I hope you'll forgive me for this one. You see the other person I wanted to be here tonight to share this great occasion isn't with us. I'm sure you've all done it, said things you regret, then realise it's too late to put them right. Well, I've done that big time and due to my stupidity I've lost the lady I admire most in this world.'

The crowd was now very silent as Andi listened in dumb dismay to Jas's dedication.

'So here it is, the one you've all been waiting for. Andi, wherever you are, I'm sorry and this is for you — *Song Of My Heart*.'

Andi hardly noticed the hand grab out at her elbow. Her eyes were transfixed on the stage as Jas began to sing.

'Sorry, Andi,' Al whispered in her ear. 'I've got to escort you from the premises.'

'No,' she tried to protest, struggling with the security guard. 'Al, please, let me hear Jas. It's my song.' He proved too strong for her, and the next moment she was being manhandled out of the forest.

She blinked in the glare of the spotlights from the stage and put a hand to her eyes to shield them.

'Nice one, Charley.' Andi heard Al's voice in her ear. 'Never thought she'd be hiding out in the bushes.'

She lowered her hand and looked into Charley's grinning face. 'You, what are you doing here?' Andi demanded.

'You didn't think I was going to miss the concert, did you?'

'But I've got your ticket. How did you get in, and the booking?'

'VIP, that's me,' Charley indicated his gold badge, then assumed a look of innocence, 'and what booking exactly was that?'

'You set me up,' Andi accused him.

'Yup,' Charley didn't look in the least repentant. 'Fooled you too, didn't I?'

One or two people began to glance over at the disturbance, but nearly everyone's attention was on Jas's performance.

'There's no need to throw me out, Al, I'm leaving.'

'Actually, you're not allowed to leave either,' Charley pointed out just as a small human torpedo hurtled herself into Andi's arms and threatened to topple both of them over.

'Andi!' it squealed.

'Ssh,' Al admonished Holly, 'do you want to get me into trouble?'

'Misty,' Holly jumped up and down taking absolutely no notice of the security guard, 'over here.'

The next moment their ranks were swelled as Misty raced over, followed at a more dignified pace by Ivy and Harry. Somehow the little group all managed to manhandle Andi up the rickety steps and into the wings.

'Will you let go of me,' Andi implored as what seemed to be about a dozen pair of hands restrained her.

'You look absolutely dreadful,' Misty said before delivering an enormous kiss. 'What on earth are you wearing?'

'Her coat smells too,' Holly wrinkled her nose, 'just like Mr Rabbit's hutch.'

'Come on, love, take it off,' Ivy advised her. 'You can't go on stage dressed in that old thing.'

'On stage?' Andi began to struggle in earnest now as her jacket was ripped off her shoulders. 'I'm not going on stage.'

'Yes, you are,' Ivy insisted.

'Can't say the jeans and shirt are much better,' Misty tucked Andi's hair behind her ear. 'Honestly, the trouble you and Dad have caused me. You're worse than a pair of children. Charley's nice, isn't he?' she whispered and waved at him over Andi's shoulder. 'Now, on you go.'

'I can't. I . . .' Andi began but her protests were no match for Misty whose thump on her shoulder blades propelled Andi onto the stage as Jas came to the closing bars of *Song Of My Heart*.

'He's singing it for you, Andi,' Misty called after her, 'you might at least say thank you.'

The crowd whooped in delight as a totally off balanced Andi fell into Jas's arms.

'Andi?' his voice was hoarse from all the singing and his shirt was soaked. 'What are you doing here? I didn't think I'd ever see you again.'

'I suppose I couldn't stay away,' Andi

310

admitted, not caring that thousands of pairs of eyes were watching them.

'Turn the microphone off, Dad,' Misty called out from the wings. 'You don't want us all to hear do you?'

He looked up and with tired eyes smiled at his daughter. 'I don't mind if you don't mind. Andi, if the only way to stop you leaving is to ask you to marry me, will you marry me?'

The cheer that went up drowned Andi's reply, but from the look of delight on Jas's face, everyone knew her reply had been yes.

THE END

We do hope that you have enjoyed reading this large print book.

Did you know that all of our titles are available for purchase?

We publish a wide range of high quality large print books including:
Romances, Mysteries, Classics
General Fiction
Non Fiction and Westerns

Special interest titles available in large print are:
The Little Oxford Dictionary
Music Book, Song Book
Hymn Book, Service Book

Also available from us courtesy of Oxford University Press:
Young Readers' Dictionary
(large print edition)
Young Readers' Thesaurus
(large print edition)

For further information or a free brochure, please contact us at:
Ulverscroft Large Print Books Ltd.,
The Green, Bradgate Road, Anstey,
Leicester, LE7 7FU, England.
Tel: (00 44) **0116 236 4325**
Fax: (00 44) **0116 234 0205**

THE AUDACIOUS HIGHWAYMAN

Beth James

When Sophie once again meets her childhood hero Julian, who's been sent home in disgrace, she feels that romance has made her life complete. However, her brother Tom and his friend Harry must confine Sophie to her home because highwaymen have been sighted in the area. Sophie, contemptuous of the highwayman rumours, finds that any secret assignation with Julian seems doomed to failure. Then — when she's involved in a frightening encounter with the highwayman — her life is changed for ever.